Spirit Jar

JUANITA HASSENSTAB ALCMAR

Trafford
PUBLISHING

Order this book online at www.trafford.com/07-0519
or email orders@trafford.com

Most Trafford titles are also available at major online book retailers.

Note for Librarians: A cataloguing record for this book is available from Library and Archives Canada at www.collectionscanada.ca/amicus/index-e.html

Printed in Victoria, BC, Canada.

ISBN: 978-1-4251-2115-0

Library of Congress Number: TXU1276913

We at Trafford believe that it is the responsibility of us all, as both individuals and corporations, to make choices that are environmentally and socially sound. You, in turn, are supporting this responsible conduct each time you purchase a Trafford book, or make use of our publishing services. To find out how you are helping, please visit www.trafford.com/responsiblepublishing.html

Our mission is to efficiently provide the world's finest, most comprehensive book publishing service, enabling every author to experience success. To find out how to publish your book, your way, and have it available worldwide, visit us online at www.trafford.com/10510

 www.trafford.com

North America & international
toll-free: 1 888 232 4444 (USA & Canada)
phone: 250 383 6864 ♦ fax: 250 383 6804 ♦ email: info@trafford.com

The United Kingdom & Europe
phone: +44 (0)1865 722 113 ♦ local rate: 0845 230 9601
facsimile: +44 (0)1865 722 868 ♦ email: info.uk@trafford.com

10 9 8 7 6 5 4

Acknowledgements:

I wish to express my gratitude to the following friends who helped me through this journey: my partner, Arturo, who was by my side from the beginning; Zelda, for her professional editing and terrific suggestions; the talented writers in the Pahoa, Hawaii, Writer's Circle—you gave me hope; Kasey, Kyle, Scott and Yens—you guys were great.

Dedication:

To my family, with love. You know who you are.

Chapter One

Lying on the floor of a Chevy Van, Morgan Shephard pulled the pillow from under his head, clutched it against his chest, and slithered his lean body under a frayed, gray Army blanket.

For the past week Morgan had been tent-camping in the scenic wilderness of the Pacific Northwest with his parents, Ray and Laura and his sister, Sara.

The family planned on spending the next two days at an isolated mountain campground—where it all began.

Cloudless fall days sustained an illusion of summer, but as the jagged Cascade Mountains swallowed the sun, a chill sifted through the forest like an invisible shroud. Evening fires of dry twigs and branches crackled and hissed as pitch drizzled onto the rock-lined fire pit.

Restless, Morgan rolled onto his stomach. He propped his forehead on his stacked hands and released a long breath.

"Gotta have something exciting to tell the guys when I get home," he told himself.

A long time passed before he hatched a plan.

"Got it!" Morgan thought. "I'll psych the guys out. Like, I borrowed a dirt bike and accidentally smashed a rattlesnake flat, and bloody, slimy guts flew into my face. Or... or... a giant hairy tarantula crawled into my backpack, and I made it my pet spider. Here's a good one—just before I crashed the dirt bike, I jumped off and rolled down a hill—like in the movies. Cool stuff like that."

Morgan frowned, thinking about the night before. "I swear I heard growling, snarling, and something big prowling through the brush. The forest ranger had warned us that a few big cats had been sighted in higher altitudes. 'Use caution,' he'd said, when hiking the trails."

"I wouldn't mind seeing a mountain lion." Morgan sighed. "Dad said that was highly unlikely, though."

Drifting in and out of sleep, Morgan smiled to himself as he recalled an incident involving his sister the night before. "Sara really freaked when I put that frog by her hand and it hopped on her leg. Did she screech…what a wuss."

Yawning, Morgan stretched his tall body full-length, nearly overturning a pile of gear crammed into the back of the van. "Oops!" he whispered.

Brushing tangled chestnut-brown hair away from his hazel eyes, he scratched an earlobe, musing to himself, "Jeez, Mom had a cow when I asked her if I could get my ear pierced. 'No way', she had said, 'not while you're living under my roof.' "

Morgan thumped a fist into the pillow, muttering, "Big deal. Anyway, I wasn't serious."

Before the drone of the car engine prompted him to sleep, another thought buzzed through his mind, "When I get home, Brice and I'll meet Joe and Jon at our secret place—the cave." He smiled to himself. "Finding that hole in the cliff behind my house—pure genius. And those guys, daring me to crawl into the black tunnel at the back of the cave. Ha! Told 'em, forget it. No way. Not me. I'm not *that* crazy. Besides, we already found one scorpion under a rock." He shuddered at the next thought. "Probably a zillion others in that tunnel."

Finally, Morgan surrendered to sleep, silencing his rambling thoughts.

Ten-year-old Sara, cocooned in a royal blue sleeping bag, slept beside her brother. Her long, coal-black curls spilled from the opening. The thick fabric mounded slightly as she rolled onto her side.

At breakfast around the campfire that morning, she had announced, "I'm going to be a pilot when I grow up." She added that she and her best friend Jane made a blood pact to go to pilot school together.

Morgan had laughed. "What'd you guys do—slash your fingers open and suck each other's dripping blood?"

"Euwww, Morgan, You are sooo gross," cried Sara. She flashed her hand in front of his face, wiggling her fingers. "We just pricked our pinkies and pressed them together."

He had continued teasing, waving a spoonful of Cheerios in her face. "Hey let me know what plane you guys are flying. I'll avoid *that* one."

"You are so not funny, Morgan," said Sara. She pushed the spoon aside, spilling soggy cereal on his T-shirt. "Oops!" she snickered and said, "Soreee."

"I'll get you," said Morgan, giving her a sideways frown as he brushed the cereal from his T-shirt. "Just wait," he warned.

"Cut it out, you two," his dad scolded, ending the squabble. "Time to break camp. We have a long drive to that other campground."

That evening, the van's tires crunching over the gravel road woke Morgan, slightly.

He rolled onto his side. "Are we ever going to get there," he wondered.

A few minutes later, Ray said quietly, "We're here."

A granite boulder the size of a Volkswagen loomed in the beam of headlights. END OF THE ROAD CAMPGROUND was painted in large block letters with bloodred paint.

Laura's scalp prickled as she stared at the homemade sign. "Unique way to welcome visitors," she said in a wary tone.

Smiling, Ray said, "It's different."

Ray slowly steered past the sign into the narrow entrance, a one-lane gravel road, overarched with low-hanging pine branches that created an endless tunnel effect. Forest foliage brushing against the sides of the van gradually thinned, and the edge of the campground appeared in the headlights.

"We won't be able to see much in the dark," Laura said.

A gravel road circled the campground. An occasional campfire flickered from fire pits, scattered through the towering pine forest. Ray stopped in front of an unoccupied space. "How about this one?"

"Looks good, as much as I can see," Laura answered, staring through the open side window. "The place seems a bit deserted."

Ray cut the engine, opened the van door, and eased his six-foot frame from the seat.

"We could crawl in the back with the kids," Laura said, squinting at her wristwatch. "Not much left of this night."

"Sure, why not," Ray said.

Laura shivered in the mountain chill and snuggled her pink fleece vest around her. The moon issued shafts of pearly glow, tinged with blush, upon her pale, upturned face. "Beautiful night," she said.

Just then, loud crackling noises startled them. They both chuckled when several pinecones smacked the ground.

"Hope Big Foot didn't have anything to do with that!" Ray teased.

"Very funny," Laura said.

Morgan stirred as he felt his blanket shift. In a sleepy voice, he asked, "Is it morning yet?"

"No, sweetie. It's late. Go back to sleep," said Laura.

"Okay, see you in the morning."

Unobstructed moonlight cast the area into a surreal landscape—dreamlike.

Laura inhaled familiar, woodsy scents, which blended into the chilly wilderness night, and blew out slowly. Contentment settled over her shoulders like a silk garment.

꧁ ꧁ ꧁

During the next two days, the Shephard family will become aware that an unspoiled wilderness can be tainted.

And that a sorrowful past can hide below the surface of incredible beauty.

Chapter Two

Morgan woke at dawn. His parents and Sara were still sleeping.

Clutching his sneakers, he slowly slid the side door of the van open just enough to slip outside.

"Good thing I slept in my sweats," he thought. Shivering in the early morning mist, he zipped his Windbreaker.

He crept around the van, listening for wake up sounds. Silence. "Good," he said quietly, and jogged across the narrow road into the forest—to explore.

After a few minutes, Morgan found a path that wandered around the perimeter of the campground.

Suddenly a familiar buzzing caused him to freeze. A sound he recognized as danger.

Extreme danger.

Morgan's stomach flipped.

"Oh, oh," he breathed.

He stood motionless, his racing heartbeat pounding in his ears.

Taking shallow breaths, he moved his head inch by inch, his

eyes tracking the sound.

A few feet ahead, under a bush, Morgan spotted a large, coiled rattlesnake—ready to strike. The tip of its tale quivered. Its forked tongue whipped out between its glistening fangs.

Morgan had to force himself not to turn and run.

He backed away in slow motion, until the creature's warning system quieted, and the snake slithered out of sight.

"Whew. That was close. Too close," Morgan said under his breath.

He turned and retraced his steps, not daring to pass by the dangerous bush, just in case Mr. Snake decided to return.

"I'd better get back to camp before I get into *real* trouble," he said.

ꔷ   ꔷ   ꔷ

The delicious aroma of coffee brewing outdoors roused Laura. She stretched and slowly opened her eyes.

"Morning, Mommy. I've been waiting forever for you to wake up," said Sara.

Sara beamed a smile toward her mother. She hugged a frayed lavender, velveteen bear to her chest. A bright blue button the size of a quarter took the place of a missing glass eye. Repaired and patched, Mr. Jellybean had endured as a favorite nighttime companion since her birth.

Laura rose up on one elbow and yawned, "Good morning."

"Mommy, Daddy and Morgan are putting up our tent. Can we have pancakes for breakfast? I'm so hungry," said Sara. Sucking in breath, she asked, "Where are we anyway?"

"We're in that campground we talked about yesterday. It's called End of the Road Campground," said Laura. She glanced down, finger-combing her hair. "Good grief," she cried. "Look at this wrinkled T-shirt. Yuck. I've got to find some fresh clothes to wear."

Shifting the bear to one side, Sara frowned at a large chocolate stain on the sleeve of her yellow sweater. "Oops!" she cried. After an exaggerated sigh, she said, "Oh…Mommy, we're *camping*. We don't need to dress up you know."

"You're right, sweetie," said Laura. She winked at Sara adding, "Besides, it's not camping unless we had SOME dirt spend the night with us."

Sara giggled, "You're funny, Mommy."

"Think so, huh?" She gave Sara a broad smile, hugged her knees to her chest, and peered through the windshield. "Your daddy is wearing his favorite camping outfit."

Orange-ribbed socks peeked over Ray's scuffed high-top leather boots. His iridescent orange parka glimmered as he moved around the blue and yellow domed tent, hammering stakes into hard-packed soil.

"Mommy, the tent looks like a giant Easter egg!" cried Sara.

Laura chuckled. "You're right. It does resemble an Easter egg, sitting on that nest of topsy-turvy pine needles."

Ray looked up as the van's side door rumbled open. "Hey, look who's up," he said. His warm breath steamed as it collided with the chill morning air. "Hope we didn't wake you."

Laura scooted across the floor. She leaned on the edge of the open door and worked her feet into brown leather hiking boots. Smiling, she said, "You've been busy."

"Yeah, Daddy, good job," said Sara as she hopped to the ground. "May I go in?"

Ray grinned, "Sure, go ahead. Morgan, hand me that hatchet. I'm having trouble sinking this last tent stake."

Morgan's navy blue nylon Windbreaker rustled as he

handed over the hatchet. He pivoted on one foot, snapping his fingers to imaginary music.

He turned toward Laura, "Yo, Mom. What's for breakfast?"

"We won't starve, Morgan," Sara said as she crawled through the tent door.

Giving Morgan an amused expression, Laura said, "I think we can scrape some pancakes together." She stood by the fire pit warming her backside. "But first your sister and I are going to the restroom."

❧   ❧   ❧

A dirt path led to a tall, square, unpainted concrete-block building. The dark green corrugated roof popped as the metal contracted in the morning sun.

"This is it," Laura said.

Inside, icy water trickled from a galvanized iron pipe above a stainless steel sink.

"Not like home," said Laura. "But, what the heck, that's camping."

Goose bumps grew under the towel as she scrubbed her arms dry.

Sara groaned when her brush stalled in a mass of tangled curls.

"Here, let me help you," said Laura. "I'll do a braid for you."

Sara thrust both arms through the sleeves of her sweater. She tightened her shoulders around her ears and scrunched her nose as Laura worked.

"Ouch, Mommy. Are you almost done? I'm cold. Please hurry."

Scooping Sara's hair into a bunch, Laura smoothed a renegade curl into place. She glanced around. "This room *is* cold. Did you finish washing?"

"Yes," said Sara. She gathered a fistful of fabric against the tip of her nose. "Can we go now? This place gives me the creeps. It's like a cave."

At the door Laura shouted, "Good-bye." The word vibrated inside the cavernous room. She laughed and said, "Sounds just like a cave."

Sara rolled her eyes. "You are so not funny, Mommy."

❧   ❧   ❧

At breakfast, Ray dug a white plastic fork into a stack of buttermilk pancakes coated with maple syrup. He shook his head slowly as he chewed and swallowed.

"Mmm, mmm, mmm," said Ray, "I don't believe there is anyplace better to have breakfast than in a pine forest. The pungent scent of a campfire mixed with the aroma of this food could never be captured in our backyard."

Across the table, Morgan, cast Sara an impish smile. "Guess what, Sis? I almost caught a rattlesnake this morning. We could've had rattlesnake steaks too. Trust me, I was *that* close."

Sara shrugged a shoulder. "Big deal," she said. "You're just making that up."

"I - don't - think - so," said Morgan in a taunting voice.

Out of the corner of his eye, he saw his mom frown.

"Oh, oh," he thought.

"Rattlesnakes are nothing to kid around about, Son," said Ray.

"I know. I know, Dad. I remember what you said. I'm careful."

"You had better be, young man," said Laura, waving her fork in Morgan's direction.

"I believe there was a bear roaming around during the night," said Ray.

Morgan shot his dad a surprised look. "Really? How do you know?"

"This morning, when I emptied our trash into the park dumpster, I noticed long scratches on the green paint. Apparently, a large bear had tried to claw its way up the side of the steel container, looking for something to eat."

"Dang. That'd be something to see," said Morgan.

"Soon as I get the chance," he told himself, "I'm going to stakeout the dumpster and get a picture of a bear scaling that garbage dump."

"Well, that's exciting news," said Laura, setting her coffee mug down. "Ah...are we in any danger?"

"There won't be a problem with those guys as long as we lock up our food supply when we leave camp and before going to bed.

"The park ranger was there. He said not to worry. There hadn't been any problem all summer with bears *inside* the campground."

"Okay," said Laura, hesitantly. "Guess he should know."

"We've had some funny experiences in these camps," said Ray.

Sara giggled, "Remember last year, when we were eating dinner and a deer plunged into our campsite? Were we surprised, or what." She sucked a quick breath and added, "And that time we were parked with a camper in the hottest—"

"Wait," Morgan interrupted, "Let me tell it, Sara. We put on our swimsuits and stood on a rock while Dad soaked us with a garden hose. The water was super warm, just like a shower. And we slept with the camper door open all night. It was barely light when I woke up. And there was a squirrel perched on our doorstep, staring at us."

"What a night," Ray said. He chuckled. "Who knows what—"

"Anybody," Laura interrupted, "for more pancakes?" To herself cautioned, "I would rather not dwell on what creepy-crawly things could have wandered through the open door while we slept."

Morgan grinned at the memory, rolling pancakes around sausage links. "Look. Pigs in a blanket."

Sara eyed his plate. "Big deal, Morgan. Those are on practically every restaurant menu. You think you know everything."

He shrugged a shoulder. "So sue me."

"Okay, okay. That's enough," said Ray.

"But Daddy, he's a big showoff," said Sara.

Laura raised an open hand, lowering her head. "Truce," she said. "Let's have peace. Okay?"

Ray glanced at Morgan and Sara. "Say, you guys up for a fishing expedition this morning?"

"Yes!" they answered in unison.

Chapter Three

After breakfast Ray and Morgan toted a mustard-colored dinghy down a path leading to a nearby lake. Sara trailed behind carrying a small canvas bag filled with snacks.

"Have fun, guys," Laura called out. "Catch lots of fish."

She entered the tent and plucked a paperback from a stack of pillows.

A gust of wind blew through the unzipped door.

The tent shuddered.

A lone wolf howled in the distance. The primitive sound sent shivers racing up her spine.

Laura frowned, whispering, "Have to get out of here. Go to the lake."

Dread trailed her as she dashed outside. She stumbled to the picnic table bench. Grabbing a pair of binoculars, she jogged down the path to the lake.

On a knoll overlooking the water, she adjusted the binoculars with fingers stiff as wood. Scanning the lake, she spotted it. "There they are," she said under her breath.

Near the far side of the lake, the yellow dinghy bobbed

on sun-spangled water. She saw Ray rowing while Morgan trolled for fish. Sara, draped over the air-filled canvas pontoon, dangled her fingers in the rippling water.

"They're okay, they're safe," Laura said.

"Wait a minute." Her eyes narrowed in thought, "What was going on back there?" She shuddered. "That eerie sensation…"

"Don't panic," she scolded herself, "everyone is fine."

She stood a few minutes, watching the trio in the dinghy. It troubled her that she had not been able to dismiss the urge to check on her family.

"I didn't get much sleep last night," Laura said quietly, "I'm tired and overreacting. That's it—a phantom intuitive nudge." She smiled to herself, "Well, that's a relief."

Back in camp she decided to spend the rest of the morning by the lake. She slid a visor over her hair, picked up a recliner, and hiked down the trail.

❦   ❦   ❦

Rousing from a nap at the sound of familiar voices, Laura opened sluggish eyelids. She saw Sara, perched in the dinghy like a queen, waving to her while Morgan and Ray tugged the small craft out of the water.

Morgan called out, "Yo, Mom. We caught our limit—trout. Big ones!"

Sara stood by Laura's chair, holding a string of rainbow trout. "Daddy said I did a good job sticking worms on the hook," she said. Scrunching her nose she added, "They felt yucky at first." Separating two of the fish from the group, she said, "I caught these."

"Well now, good job," said Laura. She rose from her chair.

"Baked fish for dinner—sounds good to me."

"Gimme," said Morgan, grabbing at the string of fish.

"Take 'em," Sara said and ran ahead.

"Meet you guys in camp," Ray called out as he tied a rope from the dinghy to a tree.

At their campsite, Ray patted the chair seat next to him. "Let's relax a bit," he said, "and let the kids handle cleaning our catch."

She nodded and sank into the seat. "Okay, you heard Dad. Get busy and clean those beauties." Leaning back in her chair, she added, "And please," she said in a tone that caught Morgan's attention, "make sure they are super clean before you wrap them in foil."

Morgan grinned and gave her a thumbs-up. "Not to worry, Mom. We'll do a good job. Right, Sis?"

With an air of authority, Sara answered, "Hey, we're professionals."

Ray reached over and caressed Laura's hand. He thought she looked peaked. "What say we rest for awhile after lunch?"

"Sounds fabulous."

Laura gazed into Ray's tanned face, musing to herself. "Should I share my strange morning with him?"

"Not yet," she decided. "Besides, nothing happened."

To no one in particular, Laura asked, "Whose turn is it to prepare lunch?"

Sara pressed an index finger to her bundled lips. Propping a hand on a slightly jutting hip, she said, "Think it's my turn."

"Great," Laura answered. "You'll find enough leftovers in the cooler."

Morgan lobbed a paper bag bulging with fish remains into a garbage can. "YES!" he cried.

Dipping his hands into a pail of water, he flicked water droplets toward Sara.

"Mommy, make him stop. He's soaking me," said Sara.

"That's enough, Son," said Laura.

"Okay," Morgan sighed as he dropped to the picnic table bench. "Hey, shrimp. How long till lunch? Sometime in this decade!"

Giving him her best scowl, Sara answered, "You are so not funny, Morgan."

Rummaging through the cooler, Sara pulled out plastic containers in rainbow shades. She circled them in the middle of the table on a doily of golden oak leaves. A frosty bottle of cranberry juice substituted as a centerpiece.

"Lunch is ready," Sara announced.

Laura stood by the table admiring Sara's efforts. She smiled, nodding toward the decorations, and said, "Nice touch."

Scrubbing his palms together, Morgan quirked an eyebrow toward the collection of lunch surprises. "Yeah, Sis," he teased, "is this a grab bag party?"

"Give your sister a break," said Ray. He pulled Sara to his side and squeezed a light hug. "Looks good, princess. Let's eat."

Sara shot Morgan a "nanner, nanner" look.

"Dad and I need to rest after lunch," Laura said as she pried the lid off one of the containers. "Yummy. I got potato salad."

"Mommy, do we have to rest too?" Sara asked. "I'm not tired."

"I guess not," said Laura. She paused a moment. "I have an idea. Morgan, when you finish eating, get the hammock and help Dad string it up between those trees," she said, gesturing with her plastic fork, "by the tent. You guys may change your mind about that nap. I thought we could go hiking this afternoon."

"Outstanding! I'm ready now," Morgan said.

Slowly shaking his head, Ray said, "You may be, but Mom and I aren't."

❧   ❧   ❧

After lunch, Sara climbed into the purple mesh cradle, clutching her stuffed bear. Swinging the hammock gently, she closed her eyes and hummed herself into a nap.

Before entering the tent, Ray glanced at Morgan, sitting at the picnic table.

"Don't wander too far. Okay?" he said.

Morgan responded with a brief wave.

He leaned his chin on the knuckles of one hand and peered at the cover of a baseball magazine, thinking, "Perfect timing and this is going to work. I'm sure of it."

Inside the tent, Laura, lying on top of a sleeping bag, greeted Ray with a lazy smile.

"Get some sleep, honey," Ray said, easing down beside her, not bothering to remove his hiking boots.

"You too," Laura answered.

Chapter Four

Morgan waited until he was sure his parents and Sara were asleep. This was his chance. And he needed to be alone for a mission—a risky mission.

He stuffed his Swiss Army knife into a back pocket and a camera into another. He filled a canteen with water and left the campsite.

Morgan figured by staying within the boundaries of the campground, he wouldn't get lost. At least he hoped not.

His mission: sneak up on a grizzly bear and take a picture. He believed this would be a seriously cool adventure-photo to share with his friends.

"I can hang out at the dumpster," he thought as he jogged away from the campsite. "If I get lucky I'll see a hungry grizzly bear. Maybe even a whole bunch."

"*And* if they act fierce, I'll just drop to the ground and play dead. Yeah, right. That's not going to work," he said under his breath. "Okay. Then I'll climb a tree!"

Arriving at his destination, Morgan crouched behind a group of forest bushes, a few feet from the campground dumpster.

He waited, glancing at his wristwatch every few minutes, checking the time.

His stomach churned from nerves—and something else.

"Am I being watched?" he wondered silently.

Morgan nervously, glanced around.

"Dang, maybe this wasn't such a good idea," he whispered.

He hunched into his jacket as the hairs on the back of his neck raised.

"I'm *not* alone," he said under his breath.

Then he saw it.

A lone coyote crept out from behind the dumpster. The animal stared in Morgan's direction.

Fear stabbed Morgan's stomach. "It sees me," he whispered as he crouched lower. "Do they attack humans?"

Soon the coyote lost interest in human prey.

Lowering its head it sniffed along the bottom edge of the dumpster.

After a moment the animal lunged toward a familiar scent. A barely audible squeak pushed from a chipmunk as the coyote pounced. Its front paws squashed the life from the small creature. The animal grabbed hold of the limp furry body with its pointed teeth, and trotted out of sight.

"Whoa! That was *gross*," Morgan said. "Sure glad that coyote wasn't stalking *me* for lunch!"

Staying as long as he dared, he left his hiding place, and followed a trail back to the campsite.

Near the tent, he stood behind a tree—listening.

His parents were still asleep.

"Whew," he uttered, "made it."

Morgan crept to the picnic table and eased onto the bench seat.

"Dang," he said, "those darn bears must not have been hungry today."

He chuckled and said quietly, "But the coyote was."

❧   ❧   ❧

A woodpecker hammering its beak into the bark of a nearby tree trunk awakened Laura.

"You awake, Ray?" she whispered.

Ray rolled onto his back. After a moment, he said, "Hmm, guess so. How long have we been asleep?"

Laura squinted at her wristwatch, "It's one o'clock. About an hour."

"We'd better get going," said Ray. "The sun will drop behind the mountains in about three hours." He tied a gray sweatshirt around his waist. From the door he asked, "Is our flashlight in my backpack?"

"I think so," said Laura. A slight frown pleated her brow. "But check anyway. The kids may have taken it out."

"Right," said Ray. He dipped his head, stepping through the tent door.

Morgan sat at the picnic table, innocently shuffling through baseball cards, thinking about his failed mission. His head bobbed to music reverberating from headphones cupping his ears.

"Hi, Daddy," Sara said. Her slight body curled around her bear, forming a giant donut in the middle of the hammock.

"Hey, princess. You comfy?'

Sara, nodded, smiling her response.

Ray lifted an earphone and said into Morgan's ear, "You ready for a hike?"

"Yo, Dad. Sure I'm ready." Morgan said, scooping off the

headset. "Your backpack's right here, and I filled our water bottles." He flashed Ray a broad smile. "I was thinking, maybe we could hike to that river we saw on the map and search for arrowheads."

"I suppose," said Ray, hoisting his backpack over a shoulder. "Good a place as any to explore. We should be back here before it gets too dark though."

"No problem, Dad."

Sara, squirmed out of the hammock.

"Everybody ready?" Laura asked as she shrugged into a red knit sweater. "Sara, would you get some fruit and grahams out of the cooler and put them in my backpack? Oh, and where is our first aid kit?"

"I've got it, Mom," Morgan said. He patted his backpack. "In here."

"Thanks, my dear," said Laura.

Morgan disappeared into the tent. "Anyone seen my sweatshirt?"

Ray winked at Laura. "Is it dark blue and kind of grungy looking? You can claim it out here, if the description fits."

Emerging from the tent, Morgan said, "Hey, that's my favorite sweatshirt."

An impish smiled tinged Morgan's expression as he screwed a baseball cap onto his head, leaving the brim backward. He stuffed the sweatshirt into his backpack.

"The camp shovel," said Morgan, "bring it?"

"Good idea," Ray replied, adding, "and you're in charge of the compass."

"It's in good hands," Morgan said, pocketing the instrument.

"Guess we're good to go," said Laura.

❧   ❧   ❧

Later, after dark, when the full moon has risen over the mountain range, Morgan will begin a wondrous adventure. A peek into another reality ?

Chapter Five

The family picked their way around huge boulders, some towering far above their heads. Dense woods of pine and oak hugged the narrow hiking path. The trail ended at a field overgrown with tall dead weeds.

"Wait a minute," said Ray when they reached the other side of the field. "Better get my bearings."

He pulled a sheet of paper from his backpack and peered at a hand-drawn map. "I picked this up this morning, tacked to a pole near the restrooms."

Laura looked puzzled. "You think we're lost?"

"Give me a minute," said Ray. He scanned the drawing, then gestured toward some large boulders stacked in a tipsy pyramid. "There's our landmark, that pile of rocks. The Hawk Valley River is that direction."

Laura peered at the crudely drawn trail guide. "I wonder who charted the trails in this area?" She chuckled and nodded toward the primitive marker. "Now *that* makes a statement."

"Let's just hope they knew the area well—and sketched this map accurately," said Ray. He gave her a sly smile. "We could be wandering around this wilderness for days."

"Maybe," said Laura. She arched an eyebrow toward him and smirked. "But we have a compass."

Suspicion claimed Sara's eyes as she peered at the ground. "Are there snakes around here?"

"Yes. But I believe they mostly linger around rocky places," said Ray.

"Sometimes," thought Morgan, giving his Dad a sideways glance. "And sometimes they hide under bushes."

Laura crouched in front of Sara and said, "If you hear buzzing, like a remote-controlled model airplane engine, you know, like the one your brother has—just stand still a minute, then slowly back away from the sound. Okay?"

"Okay, Mommy, I will," said Sara. A slight frown creased her smooth brow. "But I hope I never hear *that* sound."

"Could I see the map, Dad?" Morgan asked.

He squinted at the drawing for a minute. He ran a finger along a winding line drawn in black ink.

"This is a trail leading to the river," he said. "No problem. I know the way."

"Good work, Son," said Ray.

"Well then, lead on," said Laura.

Marching ahead, Morgan called over his shoulder, "Follow me."

"WAIT," Sara yelled. "I want to come with you."

"We're right behind you, guys," Ray called out. "Stay together."

A few minutes later Morgan and Sara arrived in sight of the Hawk Valley River.

Morgan ran to a gigantic granite shelf overlooking crystal clear water. He glanced around for a way to the top and decided to climb the nearest oak tree. He clambered up the trunk, swung a leg over a good-sized branch, and scooted along until he was above the shelf. He slid from the branch and crawled to the edge where Sara stood below.

"Gimme your hand and I'll hoist you up," said Morgan. "Trust me, it's worth it."

"Okay, just don't let go," said Sara.

"C' mon," he said. "I'm not that perverse."

He eased down on his stomach, dangling both hands over the side of the rock shelf.

"What's perverse?" asked Sara.

"Kind of like being mean," said Morgan, reaching for Sara's hand.

"Oh," said Sara. She grunted as Morgan pulled slowly, and, like a mountain climber, she walked up the side of the granite slab and scrambled over the edge.

"Thanks," she breathed.

"No problem," said Morgan.

He stood up to investigate the surroundings.

"Look, Sara—upriver."

A mass of boulders piled in the middle of the riverbed created a miniature waterfall. Rainbow colors shimmered in the mist above the foam.

"Cool!" said Sara.

"Yeah," said Morgan.

"Hey, Sis, maybe we'll see bears fishing for their lunch." To himself he added, "Then I'll get my picture."

"*Bears?*" cried Sara, her eyes widening.

"Yeah. Huge, brown grizzly bears."

Morgan held his camera in shooting position, and slowly scanned both sides of the riverbank.

Nervous, that there could be bears nearby, Sara, looked back the way they had come. "There's Mommy and Daddy," she said, her tone tinged with relief. Waving her arms overhead, she called out, "We're up here."

"Don't worry, Sara, I don't see any dangerous beasts," said Morgan.

"Good," said Sara.

Laura stopped walking. "Now how did those kids get up there?"

Ray removed his cap and swiped the cuff of his sweatshirt across his moist forehead. "You can bet that was Morgan's idea."

"Boys will be boys," Laura said, propping a foot on a boulder and tightening a shoelace.

After a brief search, for another way off the granite slab, Morgan discovered an easier way to the ground.

Sara followed close behind.

Sauntering toward his parents, Morgan said, "I was just thinking…maybe Sara and I could walk upriver." He gazed at the trail, gripping the handle of the camp shovel, then chinked the blade against a rock. "You know, to search for arrowheads."

"Let's have a snack before going on," Laura said. She shrugged out of her backpack straps. "Besides, we should stay together—at least within hearing distance of each other."

"I agree," said Ray. He ran a hand around the back of Morgan's neck. "If there are arrowheads to be found, they'll wait for you."

"I know, Dad."

They snacked in the shade of a pine tree on a thick carpet of pine needles. Water rushing over the rocky riverbed inspired a tranquil mood.

Finishing his snack, Ray balled a paper towel and stuffed it into his backpack. He scanned the trail. "Guess I'm ready to move on."

Morgan scrambled to his feet. Like a race horse at the starting gate, he shot ahead, stumbling over partially exposed tree roots zigzagging across the broad trail. He regained his balance and trudged up a rocky incline.

"Wait for me," Sara called out.

"Sara, stay with your brother," Laura said.

Her arms flailing like a miniature windmill, Sara said, "Okeydokey, Mommy."

"Better get going," Ray grunted, pushing to his feet.

Laura smiled at the sight of sunbeams slanting through tall pines, hazy with microscopic forest dust.

Pea-size orange berries hung in clusters nestled in mountain foliage. Laura recognized mountain laurel shrubs bordering the far side of the forest.

"I can just imagine this place in spring," she said, placing a hand on Ray's shoulder, "with millions of buds exploding into bloom! The fragrance must be intoxicating."

"You bet," said Ray. "I do enjoy fall in the high country, though. This time of year has its own beauty." He tipped his head back and closed his eyes. "Smell that crisp scent of evergreens?"

Laura inhaled a deep breath, exhaling slowly. "Mist coating pine needles through the chilly night, blending with damp bark and oak leaves, works for me," she said, slipping her hand into his.

Morgan's voice, ringing through the wilderness, broke into their quiet conversation.

He stood on a ridge waving his red baseball cap. "Mom, Dad. We found a great place to explore for arrowheads."

"We're on our way, " Ray called out. Morgan delivered a thumbs-up and disappeared behind a curtain of shrubs.

Climbing the semi steep incline was slow, due to clumps of slippery weeds and loose rocks. Ray reached toward Laura. He grasped her hand and pulled her to him.

Silence greeted them as they crested the hill.

"Now, where did those kids take off to?" asked Ray.

Breathless from the climb, Laura sank to a boulder. She scanned the area below. "There they are. And would you look at that."

An enormous, aged juniper tree dominated a clearing beside the riverbank. Thick, gnarled branches of dark green foliage, spiked with greenish-grey berries, spread a wide circumference, dwarfing Morgan and Sara. They were hunkered over something at the base of the massive, twisted trunk. The canopy swayed and branches creaked as wind snaked through, creating a mournful wail.

Casting Laura a lopsided smile, Ray said, "Now *that's* what I call a tree."

Uneasiness fluttered through Laura. "Did I hear moaning?" she wondered.

Her disturbing morning sifted into her thoughts.

"Could whatever it was that gave me the willies have followed me…developed a voice?

"That's ridiculous," she scolded herself. Still…"

"Look," Ray said, pointing skyward.

A hawk, circling the clearing, landed on a pine branch jutting from a group of boulders cresting a hill. Its keen eyes scanned the activity under the juniper tree.

Ray gave Laura a sappy grin. "Don't believe he's interested in us for his next meal!"

"Well, now we know why this river is named, Hawk Valley River. I believe that's a sharp-shinned hawk," said Laura. She gave Ray a mischievous smile. "I read about hawks in a North American bird book. It caught my attention one day at the library."

Ray slipped his sunglasses down and peered over the frame. "Taking up a new hobby?" he asked.

Laura gazed at the noble bird. "Beautiful, isn't it?" she said. "Birds interest me. Rodents and insects are this hawk's food of choice. It will even capture a meal of small birds, weakened by injury or disease. They're easier to catch than healthy ones."

"I read somewhere that, years ago, hawks had a bad reputation for killing barnyard fowl. People put all hawks in the chicken-hawk category," Ray said. "Most are protected these days. Guess people have come to understand the role that hawks play in nature."

Laura smiled up at Ray. "Let's join our treasure hunters."

Chapter Six

"Check it out," Morgan said as his parents approached. "I think I found some real treasure." Eyes bright with excitement, he stood and handed an object to Laura.

"What on earth?" She fingered a Kleenex from a pocket and smoothed away dirt. "Could this be an authentic piece of Native American pottery?"

Ray slid the backpack from his shoulders, setting it near. He crouched, elbows on knees, fingers loosely interwoven. He nodded toward the hole. "Is that where you found it?"

"Yeah, Dad, right there," said Morgan. "I saw something near this tree. You know like a…" He shrugged staring at the empty space.

"I can't tell Dad," he told himself, "that I heard rumbling under my feet when I started digging. And the ground shivered like an earthquake. He'll think I've flipped out!"

Morgan frowned, thinking, "Funny, Sara didn't…"

He squatted beside his dad, hugging his trembling knees.

"I don't know why I dug there, Dad," he said.

A shudder crept up his spine. "Dang," he thought, "at least

everything's quiet now."

Ray didn't notice his son's tense behavior.

Morgan glanced at his dad, saying, "I scooped out dirt, and there it was, just barely covered. When I pulled the jar out, Sara spotted two arrowheads under it."

Laura examined the pottery jar's round base that tapered into a neck about an in inch in diameter.

"There's a couple of chipped places around the opening," she said. "I'll sponge it off."

Squatting on the river bank, Laura submerged the jar into the water. The pottery radiated heat against her cool hands. A shiver crawled up her spine. She cradled the jar in her dripping palms. Feeling lightheaded, she leaned against a boulder for support.

"Okay," she whispered, "take a deep breath."

"Are you okay, honey?" Ray asked as he approached.

She stood, with his help. "I'm fine, just a moment of... maybe I'm hungry."

Ray fixed her with worried brown eyes. "You look a little pale. We'll rest a bit. There's trail mix—"

"Great," she interrupted. "Here, take this." She placed the aged pottery jar in his outstretched hand.

Ray's eyes narrowed, peering at a faint design. "Kinda looks like bird wings," he said. "Hmm, can't tell though. Too faded."

"This is going to sound strange," Laura said, hesitantly, "but did the pottery jar feel warm to you?"

Ray gave her a questioning look. "Warm?" He fingered the rough opening.

"Never mind," Laura said. She shrugged, "For a moment...I thought...guess I was mistaken."

Morgan joined his parents. He laced his fingers behind his head. "This is so cool," he said.

Feeling left out, Sara said, "Mommy, see what else we found?" She thrust a dirt-smudged hand forward. Two obsidian arrowheads lay in her open palm.

"Oh my!" Laura cried.

She bent over and cradled Sara's hand for a closer look. "These are beautiful," said Laura as she lifted one and fingered the serrated edge. She nodded toward the jar. "I believe we are looking at authentic pieces of history, guys."

Laura closed her fingers around the arrowheads a moment. "If only they could tell us…somehow communicate." A smile tugged at the corner of her mouth. She opened her hand. "Silly me," she murmured.

"There is a story molded into this jar," said Ray. "And you can bet those arrowheads saw some action." He pulled a package of trail mix from his jacket pocket and handed it to Laura. "But we'll never know."

Morgan's vision blurred.

The jar smeared into a formless blob.

He rubbed his eyelids.

Blinked.

He suddenly felt the need to hold his treasure, to assure himself that the pottery had not melted.

"Dad, could I see?"

"Sure, Son, here you go. Since you found the jar, why don't you take charge of carrying it in your backpack?"

"Thanks. I can handle it," said Morgan.

The palms of his hands tingled as he held the treasure jar. Momentary sensations of loss and sadness fluttered through his gut.

"Jeez, get a grip," he told himself. "It's just an old pottery jar. And nothing weird happened when you found it. Okay?"

In a flash, Morgan's excitement of finding treasure returned.

"Wait a minute, Morgan," said Laura. She untied a red bandana from around her neck. "Here, wrap it in this."

Sara tilted her head, squinting in the afternoon sunlight. "May I carry the arrowheads in my backpack, Daddy? I have a special place."

"Sure you can," said Ray.

Dust puffed as Morgan scooped dirt back into the hole.

He stood quietly for a moment—waiting. But the eerie rumbling sound did not return. And the earth did not shiver. "Great, everything's normal," he thought. "Must've psyched myself out."

"Do we have to go back to camp right away?" Morgan asked.

"What did you have in mind?" Ray asked.

"Maybe Sara and I," Morgan said as he swept the shovel in an arc, "could walk around awhile. You know, search for more arrowheads."

"Okay with me—I'm having a snack before we start back," Laura said. She slid her sunglasses down the bridge of her nose and peered over the top. "But not for too long. Okay?"

"And don't wander too far," Ray said.

Laura gestured toward a large boulder near the rugged, weather-beaten trunk of the juniper. "Let's sit over there," she said.

Easing onto the hard, bumpy surface, she took a deep breath. "You know, I feel guilty, taking the jar home. It doesn't feel right somehow."

"Wish I knew how to explain," she mused to herself.

"You know, I've had thoughts about that too. Maybe that jar needs a museum home," Ray responded in a quiet tone. "I feel like we're seizing...I don't know ...something that's precious to someone."

"Maybe we should locate a nearby museum," said Laura, "for Native American artifacts found in these mountains."

Ray pulled at the brim of his cap. After a minute he said, "I have an idea. When we get home let's search the Internet for tribes that hunted and lived in this area." He shot her a smile. "Could be a project for Morgan? And if he does find information on tribes that had villages around here, he could research for the nearest city with a Native American museum and we could donate the jar."

Laura turned toward him, smiling, "What a great idea."

"What's a great idea?" Morgan asked as he wandered around the tree trunk.

"Mom can fill you in."

Morgan dropped to the ground and leaned back on his elbows.

Sara climbed onto Ray's lap. Her tone tinged with disappointment, she said, "We didn't find any more arrowheads."

Laura leaned forward with her arms folded across her thighs. "Dad came up with a plan for the pottery jar. And I agree."

His eyes wary, Morgan asked, "What?"

"How about when we get home you get on a computer and search for Native American tribes that had villages in these mountains," Laura said. "There must be a fair-size city nearby, with a Native American museum for artifacts." Giving Morgan a tender smile, she added, "You know—to preserve their history, as well as share it with us."

"Yeah, well, *that* stinks," Morgan groaned. He turned onto his side and crumpled a fallen leaf.

Laura looked askance at Morgan. "To you the idea may, as you so eloquently stated, 'stinks,' but it's a wonderful way to keep the jar safe."

"Bummer. I'd keep it safe," Morgan told himself. Aloud, his tone soft, he asked, "But could we at least keep the arrowheads?"

Sara pressed her hands against each side of Ray's face, staring into his eyes. Her bottom lip stretched wide as she uttered, "Pleeeese?"

Ray chuckled at her comical expression. Over the top of Sara's head, his eyes met Laura's warm smile.

"Sure," said Ray. "Why not?" Grasping Sara's wrists, he gently pried her hands from his face. "But let's treat them like precious gems. We'll make a sturdy display box so they won't get broken."

"Thanks, Daddy," Sara said and slid from his lap.

Morgan rolled onto his back and sat up. "Guess keeping half a treasure is better than none," he muttered.

Pushing to her feet, Laura said, "It's settled then." Hooking her thumbs in her backpack straps, she said, "I truly believe the jar should be donated to a legitimate museum—not to some unscrupulous person who would sell it to a collector for profit."

"Unfortunately," Ray responded, "that sort of thing happens. All too often."

"We'd better start back to camp," Laura said.

Ray rose from the boulder. "Why don't you lead, Morgan?"

Morgan nodded.

When they reached the ridge overlooking the clearing, Laura

said, "You guys go on." She kissed Ray's whiskered cheek. "I'll just be a minute."

"You feeling okay?" Ray asked as he reached out and caressed her shoulder.

"I'm fine," said Laura. She gave him a playful expression. "Just need a time-out."

He nodded understanding. "Okay, you two. Onward." To Laura, he said, "We won't be far ahead of you."

Laura glanced at the pine tree where the hawk had perched earlier. The bird had flown away in search of a meal. River water sluicing around boulders dented the silence.

"Is the ancient juniper guarding a secret?" she wondered silently.

At that moment, a halo of sunlight crowned the tree.

Laura smiled, gazing at the beauty below.

"Yes, there *is* something mysterious about this place," she said quietly.

She huddled into her sweater.

Laura closed her eyes a moment and said, "I can feel it."

Chapter Seven

Dusk seeped through the forest as they trooped toward camp. Morgan pretended to be a Native American brave, leading his people to their village.

Campground fires flickered through trees, and crackling logs echoed in the cool evening air as they approached End of the Road Campground.

Laura lingered a moment before entering their campsite. "It feels normal," she thought.

"But...

"It's as if uninvited guests are here," she mused in silence. *"Are we the uninvited?"*

"Stop it," she scolded herself. "Everything is fine."

Sliding the backpack from her shoulders, she said, "Guess we're all hungry after that long hike."

"I'm starved," Sara answered.

Morgan stood over the fire pit, scattering bark and wood chips onto crumpled newspaper. "Dad, can I light the fire?"

Ray dropped an armload of logs near the fire pit. He pulled off canvas gloves; dirt puffed as he slapped them against his thigh.

"Sure, go ahead. When the flames take hold," he said, nodding toward the logs, "add a couple of those. Leave space between the logs, the flames need to breath."

"Ray, could you get a bucket of water?" Laura asked.

"Sure thing."

Watching water splash into the bucket, he mused silently, "Something's bothering Laura." He sighed, turning off the faucet. "Guess she'll reveal whatever it is when she is ready."

A tongue of flame from the kerosene lantern broadcast a warm glow over a faded, red-and-white checkered oilcloth spread over the redwood picnic table.

Laura brushed her hands over the cool surface of the table covering, which had been her mother's. She smiled as a dormant childhood memory fluttered like a butterfly, skimming her heart. Dismissing her reverie, Laura asked, "Hey guys, are those coals ready? We have fish to bake."

"Yup," Morgan answered.

❦   ❦   ❦

After dinner, Sara cleared the table. A plastic bag of marshmallows swayed from her outstretched hand. "Dessert anyone?"

Laura smiled, "Of course."

"Good dinner," Ray said. "Nothing like fresh-baked trout."

Morgan ejected a prolonged burp. "Oops! 'Scuse me."

"E uwww, gross!" Sara said, her tone tinged with disgust.

"At least he said, 'excuse me,' " Laura offered.

Sara smothered the end of a slender stick with a marshmallow and dangled it over the coals, coated in gray ash. "This one's for you, Bro."

Raising his eyebrows in surprise, Morgan mimicked, "Bro!"

He threw his head back and laughed into the night sky.

"What's so funny?" asked Sara.

"From you, it just sounded weird," Morgan said. He slowly shook his head from side to side, repeating, "Bro."

Sara crinkled her nose, and said, "So. Sometimes you're weird too."

After a minute of toasting, Sara cast Morgan a satisfied grin. "See, it's perfect," she said, waving the stick in his direction.

Plucking the perfectly browned marshmallow treat from the stick, Morgan said, "Thanks, shrimp. Mine don't taste as good as yours. Guess I'll tolerate you pestering me—until I'm sick of your toasted marshmallows."

Leaning back in his chair, Morgan dropped the sweet, gooey confection into his mouth.

"I am not a pest," said Sara. In a sassy tone, she added, "Besides, yours are always burnt because you get in a hurry."

Morgan grinned and shrugged. "Yeah, yeah." He stirred a stick among the coals, sneezing as ashes scurried over the fire pit.

"Have you kids given any more thought to what we decided about the treasure jar?" asked Laura, leaning toward the fire.

Morgan slumped in his chair and gazed into the flames. "Guess I could use the library computer." Still reluctant to give up the idea of keeping the jar for himself, he added, "But I don't have to do it, like, right away."

"Probably the sooner the better," Laura said. She didn't have a clue why she said that, but she felt it was true. "These mountains must have been home to many different tribes. It will be interesting to learn who they were, don't you think?"

Shrugging a shoulder Morgan said, "Yeah, I suppose so."

Sparks swirled over the fire pit as Ray added a log.

"It's my opinion," Ray said, "that the Native Americans have a great deal of wisdom to offer. You cannot deny that they have suffered. Their villages destroyed, crops trampled and burned, broken promises and treaties—it's a wonder any of them survived." Ray slid fingers around the back of his neck and peered into the inky sky, pausing a long time before continuing.

"Not to mention war between disputing tribes," Ray continued. "And disease they had no immunity against, wiped out thousands. Forcing them onto reservations far from land where they had lived and hunted for generations—tragic." He drew a deep breath, releasing it slowly. "The relocation plan altered their lives drastically, and forever."

Laura nodded her head in agreement. "Many years ago I read a quote that I never forgot: When asked by an anthropologist what America was called before the white man came, a Native American said simply, "Ours", That quote, by Vince Deloria, Jr., always gives me goose bumps...and makes me wonder."

"Makes me wonder too," Ray said.

"Maybe the best thing we can do now," Laura said, "is respect their ancient traditions. And learn more about the people that were here long before we came along."

"I'd like to know where that treasure jar came from," Morgan said.

"Yeah, the arrowheads too," Sara added.

Quiet settled over the circled family as a full tissue-paper moon emerged.

Laura rose from her chair. "I think it's time for bed." Through a yawn she said, "It's been a long, eventful day."

Steam clouded the fire pit as Ray dribbled water over the

pinkish-gray coals.

"Dad, could we hike to that store tomorrow?" Morgan asked, casting his father a questioning look. "What did that ranger call it? Oh yeah—Red Bear General Store." He rushed on, "We need worms. And we haven't tried marshmallows yet." Snapping his fingers, he chanted, "Worms and marshmallows, wow, what a treat!"

Ray chuckled and said, "Morgan, my man, you are entertaining." While he shifted the drenched coals with the blade of the camp shovel, making sure the fire was extinguished, he answered, "We could hike to that other lake and try our luck there. Even go for a swim."

"That'll work," Morgan said. Through a yawn, he said, "Sounds great."

"Good," said Ray.

After the sleeping bag zippers slid closed and the pillows were fluffed and bunched, Ray asked, "Are you guys settled now?"

Both youngsters answered muffled, "Uh-huhs."

"Sara, do you have a flashlight in case you have to chase a wild animal away from our door?" Laura teased.

"Oh, Mommy. I'm not scared," said Sara.

Morgan rose up on his elbows. In a devilish tone, he said, "Sara, that forest ranger did say cougars had been spotted in these mountains."

"That's enough teasing, Morgan," Laura said in a firm tone.

"Okay," he sighed.

Morgan's vision blurred as he stared at the dark image of the treasure jar, nestled in the folds of a towel near his feet. "Not again," he thought.

But drowsiness tugged his eyelids closed before the jar

turned into a blob, like before. Sleep followed quickly, allowing him to dream.

A boy clad in an animal hide that draped his waist and hung unevenly to his knees floated toward him over a weed-stubbled field. Long black braids lay over his bare chest. Morgan flinched momentarily when the boy—his features expressionless—placed a cold hand on his arm.

Suddenly, icy wind swirled around them.

The shrill, high-pitched cry of an eagle sent a violent shudder through Morgan's dreaming body.

In his dreaming mind, Morgan heard the words: "Our journey together has begun."

Morgan tried to speak, but words clogged his throat.

The dream dissolved—too soon.

Morgan awoke briefly and clamped his eyelids, hoping the dream would return.

But it didn't.

❀   ❀   ❀

At dawn, the thump of a car door closing woke Laura. "Too early," she whispered. She turned on her side and slid under the flannel lining of her sleeping bag.

A while later, Morgan's whispers and Sara's giggles woke her.

She kept her eyes closed—waiting. But the unease she felt yesterday was gone. She yawned and said, "Guess you kids are ready to get up."

"I've been awake for hours," Morgan said.

Sara sat up. "Me too."

Ray groaned as he rolled onto his back. In a sleepy tone he asked, "Is it morning yet?"

Crawling to Ray's side, Sara said, "Oh, Daddy, you know

it's morning." She gently pinched his eyebrows, forcing his eyelids open. "See? Besides, aren't you hungry?"

He lightly tweaked her nose. "You bet, princess. This fresh mountain air is giving me a great appetite."

Laura rose up on an elbow and winked at Ray. "Let's get this day started."

❧   ❧   ❧

As they ate breakfast, the morning sun warmed everything it touched. Chirping birds welcomed the day. Squirrels entertained them as they chased each other's gray, feathery tails around tree trunks.

"Did I hear mention," Laura said as she brushed bread crumbs from the tablecloth, "of a hike to the store this morning?"

"As a matter of fact, you did." Ray said, shrugging into his parka. "We could use a supply of worms. Wanna come along?"

Laura pulled a sweatshirt over her head. "Yes, I would. I'm curious about the merchandise they have to offer."

Morgan stood near the fire pit, fishing pole in hand, casting. He braced his body, reeling in the line as if he had hooked something heavy. With a hint of laughter in his voice, he said. "Whoa! Look what I caught—a pinecone."

Sara screwed up her pug nose as she buttoned a bright red sweater. "Oh, Morgan, you are such a dork. C' mon let's go."

"Yeah, great fisherman," Ray said. "Throw that monster back. Time to hit the road."

❧   ❧   ❧

Today, the family will hear an appalling tale of disease, betrayal and loss, that will explain Laura's mysterious uneasiness around End of the Road Campground.

Chapter Eight

A rock chimney perched on the gabled roof of a gray clapboard building emitted a slender stream of smoke. A sign reading Red Bear General Store, burned into a rough-hewn slab of wood, squeaked as it swung from a rusty chain fastened to the roof-line over the entrance door. Two sagging steps clung to a porch that stretched along the front of the building.

Eyeing the rustic structure, Ray chuckled. "Must have been here since the Gold Rush days."

Laura tested a step with one foot and found it remarkably solid.

Standing on the porch she said, "Just a bit timeworn."

She smiled at a wannabe bench—a decayed log, sliced in half and crudely cemented to chunks of discarded two-by-fours. A slant to the finished product, created an old-time atmosphere.

"Maybe it's a façade? You know, to pull us into a former era for a moment," said Laura. She quirked an eyebrow at Ray. "You think?"

Ray slid an arm around her waist. "It's working," he replied. "Modern conveniences—who needs 'em? Don't miss my cell phone a bit."

Elbowing his ribs, she said, "Not funny, mister."

A cowbell dangling above the doorjamb clanged as Ray opened the door. He peered over his sunglasses at Laura. An amused expression tickled his eyes.

A craggy-faced old man leaned against a back wall behind a bar that could have been salvaged from a western ghost-town saloon. He scratched his frizzy beard and grunted as he pushed from the wall. He wore his long gray hair in a ponytail.

Waving a jaunty hello, the old man said, "Come on in, folks. What can I do ya for?"

The worn oak floor creaked as the Shephard family approached. The double garage-size room carried a faint aroma of burning logs. Roasted coffee beans, sage, and cinnamon scented the air, creating a friendly atmosphere.

Morgan spotted the head of a gigantic grizzly bear mounted on the wall behind a black potbelly stove. Inside, lazy flames licked the oval glass inserted in the door. "Did you shoot that bear?" he asked.

"Naw, son," said the man. "Can't recollect how that come to be hangin' there. I couldn't shoot an animal." He winked at Laura. " 'Cept maybe a pesky raccoon. And I ain't so sure 'bout that even."

Ray issued a throaty chuckle, enjoying the old man's gentle manner of speaking. He asked, "Have you lived in this area a long time?"

Folding his arms across his red and black plaid flannel shirt, he responded, "Well now, let's see. Guess it's been near fifty years since me and my dear departed Bessie moved up here right after we were married. My grandfather left this place to me." His eyes misted in reflection. "A local carpenter and I built the cabin you see out back. That dear woman's been gone 'bout five years now." He massaged an earlobe as if for comfort.

"There was a mining town 'bout a mile from here. Our store kept the folks working there supplied in necessities. Soon's the gold vein petered out, folks packed up and left."

Morgan's eyes held curiosity. "Is it a ghost town now?"

"Naw, son he replied. "A few years ago, a forest fire took what buildings were standin'." He paused in recollection. "My name's Mr. Harold, by the way."

"We're the Shephard family," said Ray.

Laura picked up a light brown basket, admiring the woven design. She smiled at Mr. Harold.

"Are these made by Native Americans from this area" she asked. Holding the basket toward a shaft of light from a small window, she said, "This is really beautiful."

"We get 'em from a community not far from here. They bring me a few every summer. Seasons over now. You're holding the only one left. Wanna buy it? Sure'd make the basket weavers happy."

"Yes, I would," said Laura. "I collect baskets." She tucked a dark curl behind an ear. "By the way, could you tell us some of the history of this area?"

She hesitated.

"I'm curious about the campground, how long it's been there," Laura said, trying to sound offhand. "It's such a beautiful area. We were lucky, I guess. The place is almost empty." Shrugging, she added, "Maybe because it's the end of the summer."

"That campground just sprouted, a long, long time ago," Mr. Harold said, knuckle-scrubbing his whiskered cheek. "Guess folks needed a resting place after a day of fishing. Weren't nothing fancy back then." He cast Laura a half-smile. "State parks took it over couple of years ago. Bulldozed a road so people could drive into the place. Even supplied a restroom, picnic tables and fire pits."

Taking a long time before continuing, he sank onto a tall wooden stool and leaned an elbow on the bar. His gray, bushy eyebrows melded in a frown. "Well now, I wouldn't wanna scare these youngsters of yours. But, by gum, there's a tale 'bout that campground and if y'all wanna hear—"

Before continuing, Mr. Harold arched an eyebrow toward Ray and Laura. A questioning expression glazed his bright blue eyes.

Curious to hear Mr. Harold's tale, Laura answered, "Why not?"

She looked over her shoulder at Sara, sitting cross-legged in a wooden rocking chair examining cloth Native American dolls. "I just wanted to make sure she wouldn't hear," she said to Mr. Harold. "I don't want to frighten her."

Morgan pressed against the bar counter and stacked his hands under his chin. "Please, Mr. Harold. Tell us."

Harold adjusted his chunky body on the stool. In a slow drawl, he began to spin the legend of the White Feather tribe.

"Folklore has it that the campground was established over a Native American tribe's village. They were of Sanpoil heritage, 'bout thirty in number, so the legend goes. Well, a couple of fur trappers showed up one day to do some trading. Seems one was carryin' pox." Sadness claimed his eyes as he rubbed the side of his gray whiskered cheek. "Smallpox," he said quietly.

Mr. Harold paused a long time before continuing. "Contagious as all get out. Anyways, guess one took sicker'n a dog and couldn't leave the village. His partner hightailed right outa there, leavin' his friend behind. Next thing, Indians started getting sick. Legend has it the trapper notified the doctor in that mining town down the road 'bout his friend lookin' bad—fever, talkin' out of his head and such. The doc round up a sheriff to go along, case of trouble."

Mr. Harold pulled a pipe from his shirt pocket. Staring over the heads of his listeners, he rubbed the smooth cherrywood bowl with his gnarled, arthritic fingers.

Morgan shuffled from one foot to the other, anxious for the story to be continued. He took a sip of the soft drink Mr. Harold had offered and asked, "What happened next?"

"Well, you see," Mr. Harold began, "by the time them two reached the village, things was real bad. Prit' near everyone dead or dying. Doc did what he could."

Slowly shaking his head, Mr. Harold sighed. "But weren't much he could do for those poor souls. The sheriff ordered every teepee burned, including everything in 'em. Must have been a doozie of a bonfire."

Mr. Harold inhaled deeply, and slowly exhaled, puffing his cheeks.

"And the dead…nothing to do but bury 'em in a mass grave, before things got too…" He looked askance at Laura. "Sorry, Ma'am, but you can imagine. Doc and the sheriff stayed till—"

Eager for more details, Morgan broke in, "Then what happened?"

Mr. Harold drank from a glass of water before answering.

"Well, ya see, story goes there were three survivors." He peered at Morgan over his bifocals. "Chief White Feather, his grown son and a lad 'bout thirteen, believed to be the chief's grandson. Now don't that beat all? Seems they were out scouting for game. Winter comin' on an' all. The three of 'em showed up in time to see nothing but a huge smoldering heap of ashes, the sheriff overseein' the whole kit'n caboodle. The chief didn't understand what happened to his people, everything gone an' all. In town, details of the whole tragic story was translated to the survivors, with the help from a local who spoke the Native American language, of this tribe.

"After the meetin', folklore has it, Chief White Feather never spoke a word. All three survivors just mounted their horses and rode back to their destroyed village."

A sorrowful expression leaked into Mr. Harold's eyes as he went on. "Folks swear they could hear relatives and friends keening for the dead for days. This is where everything gets kinda fuzzy. Seems this tribe had a funeral ritual, and those folks were denied tradition. Because of this, all those souls, or spiritual beings, were in torment—lost." Slowly shaking his head, he said, "It had to have been a sad, confusing time for those survivors."

He removed his wire-rimmed bifocals and wiped the lenses, using his shirttail. His hands trembled slightly as he adjusted the earpieces.

"You understand," said Mr. Harold, "this here legend's been told again and again, so's it may been gloried up a bit." Tapping the bowl of his pipe against the scarred edge of the counter, he added, "But my guess is, most is true."

Mr. Harold looked in the direction of the campground.

"You know, locals have a name for that place. They call it

'Spiritville.'"

Laura's scalp prickled. She began to put everything together. The strange feelings she experienced around their campsite were clear to her now. *Ghosts from the tragic incident of years ago were there to grieve over the loss of the ancient burial tradition.*

And somehow, their sorrow had penetrated her psyche.

Wrapping her arms around her waist to control her trembling hands, and breathing slowly to calm the churning in her stomach, Laura waited for Mr. Harold to reveal what she already knew.

Ray felt Laura shudder. He circled an arm around her shoulders asking, "Can you fill us in on why or how the campground earned such a name?"

Morgan clamped his lips, pinching off questions eager to escape. "This is way too cool," he thought. He adjusted his arms on the bar. Anxious to hear more, he urged, "Tell us, Mr. Harold. Tell us everything."

Mr. Harold responded in a voice harboring a question. "Well, now if it's okay with your folks…"

He quirked a bushy eyebrow toward Laura for her response. Getting a slight positive nod, he continued.

"This part's a little uncertain," said Mr. Harold, "but legend has it that this tribe believed that after death, souls could go to the land of the dead at the end of the Milky Way. Or the soul could be transformed into a ghost and remain on earth." He paused a moment before adding. "I'm trying to recall the belief as I heard it years ago."

Adjusting his glasses, Mr. Harold continued. "Something eerie—ghosts or spiritual beings—visit the campground this time every year, like clockwork.

"By the way, the mass grave was never marked as a memorial to those poor souls." Mr. Harold sighed. "The exact location—unknown."

He rose from the stool and popped the pipe stem into his mouth, using an index finger to tamp fresh tobacco into the bowl. With his free hand he struck a match under the bar top.

After a few puffs he said, "That's just about it, folks."

More puffs.

"Now you know why there's not much company," said Mr. Harold, gesturing toward the campground with his pipe, "up yonder."

Rubbing his icy palms together in swift motion, Morgan said, "*OhmiGod!* There are ghosts floating around us!" Jamming his fists into his sweatshirt pockets, he asked, "Mr. Harold, what kinds of spooky things have you heard about?"

Laura looked over her shoulder at Sara, cradling a Native American doll in her arms, singing the ABC ditty.

"Well, like you said, Mr. Harold," Laura said with a smile, "I'm sure the legend has been embellished with a bit of…fantasy over the years."

Mr. Harold sensed Laura wanted his cooperation in her assessment. He sucked on the pipe stem a few times. Striking a relaxed pose, he slumped back on his stool.

"Oh sure, missus. True enough," he said. "Legends are usually full of all kinds of made-up stuff."

"Sure makes a great story, though," said Ray. He issued a throaty chuckle. "Legends are legends, you know? Well, we better get what we came for."

Morgan sensed Mr. Harold was definitely avoiding an answer to the question of ghost sightings. He scrunched his mouth into a bunch to show his disappointment. "Bummer," he thought. "Guess I won't get any real good stuff about ghosts." Undaunted, he tried another question: "Mr. Harold, have you seen any ghosts around your store?"

Patting Morgan's shoulder, he responded, "Naw. No ghosts 'round my place.

"Y' all rest easy now. Nothing dangerous around that campground. Just something in the air, you might say." He chuckled, offering a plate of cookies. "Anyway, folklore's supposed to feed our imaginations."

"We'd better get what we came for," Ray urged again. "We need worms and a package of those miniature marshmallows for bait. Oh, Mr. Harold—what's the name of that lake east of the campground?"

"That's Crystal Lake. Some good fishin' there, by gum."

"Great," said Ray.

꿍   꿍   꿍

Relief flooded Laura as they left for the campground. Now she understood the reason for her uneasiness. "Of course," she thought. "It's the time of year for the ghostly visitation!"

She turned toward Ray as they reached their campsite and whispered, "I've got something to tell you." Laura tucked her hands into her pockets. Caution flickered in her eyes. "Later— when we're alone."

Ray reached out and squeezed her shoulder, "Got it," he said.

Chapter Nine

Morgan slouched in a chair, thinking, "I've been cheated. Haven't seen anything spooky. The old man's probably right about the legend being part true. Dang, sure would like to *see* a ghost, though."

Morgan puffed a sigh. "And time is running out," he muttered under his breath.

"Dad, when are we going to that Crystal Lake?" he asked, jabbing a stick into ashes inside the fire pit.

"How about after lunch?" Ray answered, "We have fresh bait."

"We could pack a picnic lunch," said Laura. "No reason why we can't go now."

"Sounds like a plan," said Ray.

"Great," said Morgan. "Swimming too?"

"Of course," answered Laura as she crouched beside a cooler, sitting on the rocky ground under a barberry bush.

"That'll be fun, Mommy," exclaimed Sara.

"Need any help, honey?" Ray asked.

"Yes," Laura said, pulling packaged food from the cooler.

"You could get a blanket from the van." Filling a picnic basket, she added, "Swimsuits and towels are in that tote beside my sleeping bag."

"Got it covered," said Ray.

Morgan disappeared into the tent. "Sara, don't come in here. I'm busy."

Sara rolled her eyes. "Mommy, could I wear my swimsuit under my clothes?"

"Sure," said Laura.

Ray peered at the hand-drawn trail map. "There's a path to Crystal Lake," he said, pointing toward a stand of pine trees behind the tent, "in that direction."

A few minutes later, Ray asked, "Is everybody ready?"

"Yo, Dad," said Morgan as he started toward the trail. "I'll lead."

Sara jostled her way around her brother, and slipped ahead of him. "I want to," she said. "You get to lead all the time."

Morgan shoved her aside, throwing her off balance. She landed on her knees in the underbrush.

"Oops!" said Morgan. "Didn't mean…"

"Morgan!" Ray called out. "Watch the rough stuff."

"But Dad, she's not experienced at following hiking trails," said Morgan. He gave Sara a "you're not hurt" expression. "Besides, it was an accident."

Laura helped Sara to her feet, brushing debris from her sweatshirt. "You can lead on our way back, honey. Okay?" Glancing at Morgan, she said, "Your brother didn't do it on purpose."

"Guess so," said Sara, frowning at Morgan. "But he's a jerk."

꧁ ꧁ ꧁

The trail, partially hidden at times by low-growing underbrush, wandered through the dense pine and oak tree forest.

As they neared their destination, the trees parted, revealing tawny-colored bunchgrass layering a sloped bank into Crystal Lake. Spikes from the autumn sun, resembling Fourth of July sparklers, skipped over the rippling surface.

"This is nice," Laura said. Nodding toward the lake, she added, "It appears we're alone."

She spread the blanket over a thick, spongy layer of pine needles that had lain undisturbed for years. "Anybody hungry?"

"I can wait," Ray said. "Been snacking on trail mix." He squirmed out of his sweatshirt. "Hey, Morgan, my man. Bet I can beat you into the water."

Morgan laughed at the challenge, saying, "No way."

He stripped down to his swim trunks in record time and sloshed into the water a second ahead of Ray. Using both hands he propelled forward.

The floor of the lake dropped suddenly.

Morgan gulped air just in time—before he disappeared.

Chapter Ten

Laura felt her heart contract at losing sight of Morgan.
Her breathing quickened.

Tears stung her eyes as she scanned the sparkling water.

But Morgan had not surfaced.

"Ray, where's Ray?" she whispered, "under water too?"

At that moment, Morgan's head popped from the surface.

Ray's, a second later.

"Finally," Laura breathed. "Relax. he's a good swimmer," she reminded herself.

She turned her attention to Sara.

Clutching a towel around her shoulders, Sara asked, "Mommy, could I practice swimming?"

"Sure, honey. The water may be a bit chilly though."

Laura shivered as she waded through crystal clear, shallow water. "I can see where the lake got its name," she said.

Undaunted by the cold, Sara shrieked and paddled in circles.

In the middle of the lake, Morgan tread water. Taking a deep breath and holding it, he plunged. Keeping his eyes open, he scissors kicked downward.

Several shiny, spinning objects caught his attention.

Curious, Morgan swims toward them.

Chrome fishing lures the size of tablespoons, without handles, sway with the lazy current.

A school of baby trout scooting along, distracts him a moment.

Morgan feels something like feathers brush against his legs.

He looks down.

Nylon fishing line, is wrapped around his ankles—trapping him.

Fear spills through his gut.

Morgan clamps his eyelids, hoping for a miracle.

Heartbeats like thunder pounds his ears.

Panic rips through his mind as he struggles to free himself.

His lungs burn. He needs air. *Fast!*

Then, it happens.

Chapter Eleven

Morgan feels icy fingers curl around his forearm, and yank him swiftly upward.

Like magic, the binding around his ankles melts.

Breaking the surface, Morgan gulps air.

He inhales a few deep breaths to calm his pounding heart.

He looks around for his rescuer.

Nobody is there, except his father, a few yards away.

Treading water, Ray calls out, "Are you okay, Son? I was about to go after you."

"I'm good, Dad," Morgan sputters, and swims toward shore.

"Did I imagine what happened down there?" he wonders silently.

He wasn't ready to admit that he was in *big* trouble—down there. And that some mysterious underwater creature had saved him.

"There's your daddy and Morgan," said Laura, squinting into the afternoon sun. "They're on the way back." Reaching for a towel, she said, "And I think you've had enough swimming for today." She laughed. "Your skin resembles a plucked chicken."

Sara giggled at her mother's description. "Okay," she said through chattering teeth.

Morgan dismissed his strange underwater experience from his mind, for the moment. At least until he could be alone to think.

"I'm hungry, Mom," Morgan said. "Can we eat now?" Morgan glanced at Sara, snuggled in Ray's flannel shirt. "What's wrong with you, shrimp face?"

"Nothing," Sara said as she narrowed her eyes. "Stop calling me that. It sounds stupid."

"Morgan," Ray warned.

He shrugged a shoulder, and sank to the blanket, casting a smirk in Sara's direction.

"If she only knew what just happened to me," he thought.

"Let's see what we have for lunch," said Laura. She held up a plastic bag of sandwich buns and tossed it to Morgan.

"We have sliced turkey, cheddar cheese, and fruit salad I bought at Mr. Harold's store.

Sara, sitting cross-legged, leaned forward and asked, "No marshmallows?"

"Yeah right, Sara," said Morgan. He reached over and lightly tweaked her nose. "We don't have a fire, silly."

She batted his hand away, "*Duh*, I know that!"

"Now, now guys," Laura said. "I'm a little unnerved this afternoon, so give me a break. Make nice, okay?" Peering at Morgan over her sunglasses, she said, "I believe she was teasing."

"Okay. Whatever," Morgan said. He began stacking meat and cheese on a bun. "Great idea, Mom."

"Got a headache, honey?" Ray asked, scooping salad onto a paper plate.

Laura leaned back against a tree trunk. Sighing, she said, "Not yet."

Gesturing with a carrot stick toward the lake, Morgan said, "Look over there, Sara—a path. We could take a walk around, the lake after lunch."

In a wary tone Laura said, "I don't know about that, Morgan." A slight frown pleated her brow. She peered into the distance. "We don't know how far or where the path leads."

"Mom's right, Morgan," Ray agreed. "We'll all go for a walk after lunch."

Through an exaggerated sigh, Morgan answered, "Okay, Dad."

Ray turned toward Laura. "Are you up for it?"

"Sure," she answered, biting into an apple.

Strolling on the narrow path around the lake, Laura confided in Ray about the anxiety and eerie sensations she suffered in the campground. And that she must be sensitive to the sorrow surrounding the demise of the White Feather tribe.

She turned her anxious eyes toward Ray's profile and said, "This must sound crazy to you. But, I know what I felt. And to me it was real."

They stopped walking. She gazed at the children a few yards ahead, crouched over something of interest.

Ray grasped her shoulders gently and turned her to face him. He lifted her chin and looked into her eyes. "You know what? I believe in your sensitive nature," he said.

Giving Ray a warm smile, she said, "I guess my intuition was nudging me."

Morgan's shout broke into their moment.

"Dad, Mom! There's a dead frog lying flat on its back, and big black ants are carrying pieces to a nest." He pointed toward a large pyramid of fine dirt. "Millions of 'em—you gotta see this!"

"Okay, we're coming," said Ray. He smiled into Laura's eyes, "Would you like to see nature at work, my love?"

Laura breathed deeply, relaxing her shoulders. She exhaled slowly, releasing pent-up emotions. She chuckled, then said, "Why not?"

∞　　∞　　∞

As they huddled around the campfire that evening, Laura sensed the mysterious, unsettled mood had quieted.

"The spirit ghosts are at rest," she mused to herself.

She shivered and snuggled into her jacket, "At least, I hope—until next year."

"Could the mass grave be under *our* campsite," she wondered. "*OhmiGod!* what a horrible thought."

Elbows on knees, Morgan leaned toward the fire, thinking "What did happen to me this afternoon? Could a monster octopus be living in that lake? Whoa! That's a scary thought. But it had a hand—icy-cold hand…

"Well whatever it was, saved me," he reminded himself silently.

"You know, Morgan said, "some of that stuff about the Chief White Feather legend could be real." Poking a stick into the coals, he added. "Anyway, sounds true."

Sara looked at her brother and asked, "What's true?"

In a nonchalant tone Laura interjected, "Oh, just some story the old gentleman at the store told us. We can talk about it tomorrow."

Shrugging a shoulder, Sara said, "Okay."

Ray turned to Morgan and cast him a confiding wink. "We sure had a great day. The water wasn't too cold for this late in the season."

"Okay, okay," Morgan thought. "I got the message—don't be an idiot and scare your sister."

Smiling to himself he thought, "They would all freak, if I told them what happened to me today."

Morgan turned his attention to toasting a marshmallow. "Do we have to go home tomorrow? Can't we stay one more day?"

Ray rose from his chair and lay a small log on the red coals. "We've had a great trip, but we must leave tomorrow." He turned toward Sara and said, "Hey, princess, toast one of those for me."

Laura's nylon jacket rustled as she leaned forward to catch warmth from the fire. "It's time to get home," she said quietly.

"Bummer," said Morgan.

Late that night, Morgan lay awake, trying to recall a dream he had the night before.

"I was in a field," he mused silently, "Yeah. I remember now, a boy my age was there too."

He yawned.

Rolling onto his side, he closed his eyes. Soon he was asleep and dreaming.

Wandering alone, through a dark forest, Morgan crept toward hazy light flooding a clearing.

A tap on his shoulder shot fear through his body. Cautiously he turned around.

Behind him, the Native American boy from the other dream

stood, smiling. He nodded toward the curtain of darkness edging the pool of light.

"Come," the boy said, "it is time for adventure."

Fearful of beasts that may be lying in wait within the forest, ready to attack, Morgan tried to protest. But all he could voice were gurgling sounds deep in his throat.

"Maybe next time," the boy said and disappeared into the darkness, leaving Morgan and the dream behind.

Overnight, thick gray clouds rolled in, blanketing the mountains with a sprinkling of frost.

After breakfast that morning, Ray brushed debris from the boat with a broom. He looked up as Morgan came toward him.

"Would you pull that plug, right there? As soon as the air is out, you can help me roll it up."

Morgan knelt beside the raft. "Dad, could we row around the lake one more time?"

Ray smoothed his hand over the rounded canvas and said, "If we do, you guys have to dry the boat again."

"We will," Sara promised.

"It's still early," Laura said. "Wait, let me get the camera. I'll get a group picture of you out there."

Balancing the raft overhead, Ray and Morgan toted it to the lake.

As the trio rowed away from shore, Laura swiped a jaunty salute and called out, "Ahoy on ship!"

They all laughed and waved just as the sun peeked around a cloud, edging it with gold. Laura snapped a few shots and tucked the camera into her jacket pocket.

Morgan trailed his fingers in the dark, satiny water, musing about the Chief White Feather legend. He couldn't wait to lay that story on his friends.

A while later, gusts of wind swept across the lake, chilling the afternoon.

"Time to head back to shore," Ray said. "I believe there's a storm brewing."

෴   ෴   ෴

They broke camp quickly, while gray clouds swirled overhead.

"I think we are leaving just in time," Laura said as she buckled her seat belt. "Rain is definitely on the way. We sure had a great vacation—perfect weather."

Ray flashed her a broad smile. "You're right-on about that. Couldn't have been much better, huh, you two in the back seat?"

Morgan, snapping his fingers to music from headphones said, "Yo, Dad. Totally awesome."

Slumped in her seat, Sara snuggled a Native American doll against her chest. "I had fun, Daddy."

Dusk had settled on the landscape as they entered the outskirts of Woodlake, where the Shephard family lived.

Ray steered the van into their driveway. "We're here," he said.

Laura sighed, "Ah, home."

෴   ෴   ෴

After a pizza dinner, Morgan went to his room. He placed his backpack on the bed, unbuckled the flap, and lifted out the pottery jar. Carefully, he placed it on a shelf above his pillow.

As he toed off his untied Reeboks, he stared at the jar, thinking, "Wish I knew why it and the two arrowheads were buried together. Maybe a special ceremony?" He frowned. "And that weird rumbling and shaking. What was that about?"

Unbuckling his belt, his blue jeans slid to a heap on the floor. He dropped to his bed, rolled into a comforter, and coasted into sleep.

Laura settled Sara into bed, reading a chapter of *Tom Sawyer*.

After Sara dozed off, she peeked in on Morgan. She found him rolled into a rust-colored comforter, asleep.

The Seth Thomas clock in the living room chimed three o'clock a.m. when Morgan began to dream.

The Native American boy and he were in a canoe. Slender branches formed a frame, covered with animal skins. They were skimming through clear river water. His dream companion turned toward him, a broad smile lighting his bronze face. He waved a paddle over his head, gesturing ahead.

The dream turned into a nightmare.

Suddenly, the canoe rocked from side to side in swift current, and then spun like a top.

Morgan moaned.

Laughter from the boy exploded within the dream as he gained control and steered the canoe into a deafening roar.

Rapids!

Morgan clenched his teeth, clutching the edges of the canoe. Foam crashed over and around the boulders, partially hidden in the churning water.

The canoe dipped dangerously sideways, threatening to tip

over.

The dark-eyed boy shouted something.

Over the roar of the water, Morgan couldn't hear.

"What?" he called out in a croaking dream voice. "What did you say?" But his throat clogged over the words.

Morgan woke feeling disoriented.

"Jeez," he murmured into the pillow.

"The dream boy shouted something. But what was it?"

Groaning his disappointment, Morgan yanked the comforter over his head.

Lying motionless, he willed himself to fall asleep again, to continue the river adventure. Even if it was scary.

But he failed.

꾕   꾕   꾕

Morgan spent Sunday afternoon with his friend Brice. Before he told him about digging up the treasure jar and arrowheads, Morgan swore him to secrecy. He didn't want anyone else besides Brice and his own family to know—just yet.

He didn't share the Native American boy dreams. Or, of being saved from drowning in Crystal Lake, by a mysterious being. They were just too weird and complicated to explain.

Morgan told Brice that he heard a horrible legend about the campground and he wanted to tell the guys. So they called Joe and Jon to meet them at the cave.

He gave a colorful account of the Chief White Feather legend, adding extra gruesome details to capture their full attention.

And it worked!

Chapter Twelve

Monday morning, Morgan shuffled to the kitchen table. He wore a dark blue T-shirt that draped well below his knees. Tangled hair brushed his narrow shoulders. He had avoided haircuts all summer, thinking it would be cool to show up the first day of school with a ponytail. Cradling the pottery jar in the crook of his arm, he yawned and sank into a chair. He slid the jar to the middle of the table.

"Mom, promise not to laugh if I tell you something kinda weird?" said Morgan.

Laura, sitting at the table, sorting through a week of mail said, "Sure," she chuckled. "You can tell me anything—except something that will send me over the edge." She gave him a tender smile and ruffled his uncombed hair. "Just kidding. What's up?"

He quirked an eyebrow at her and leaned back in the chair. "This is weird, so brace yourself." He gripped his hunched shoulders. "I'm serious, Mom. Promise?"

Laura took a deep breath, letting it out slowly. "He couldn't tell me something that bad, could he?" she wondered. A wary expression claimed her eyes.

Aloud she said, "Honey, I hope you know I would never laugh at you." She added, "May laugh with you, though." She reached over, lightly squeezing his forearm.

Morgan stared at his mother's hand. The gesture reminded him of Crystal Lake and the icy hand that clutched his arm, pulling him to safety.

"That was *not* my imagination. It *did* happen," he told himself.

"Can't tell Mom about that. She'd freak!"

Laura's voice broke into his thoughts. "Honest, it's okay, Morgan. Tell me what's going on."

"Where's Sara?" he asked.

"She's at Jane's house."

Nervously jiggling his leg up and down, he thought, "Dang. Glad she's not here. Don't need that little pest around, asking stupid questions."

Staring into his clasped hands, Morgan risked embarrassment and said, "Okay, here goes."

He took a deep breath before he spoke again.

"When I hold the pottery jar—I've been calling it my treasure jar—I feel kinda funny, like a spark hits my stomach and my hands tingle."

He licked his dry lips, picked up a giant glass of orange juice, and gulped the cool liquid.

Laura kept her expression serious during Morgan's revelation. Before responding, she poured coffee into a mug.

"Well now, that's interesting."

She picked up the jar and ran her fingertips around the worn opening. "Sure would like to know something about it," she said, her tone trailing off.

"Me too," said Morgan.

Laura smiled, draining the tension from the moment. "Don't you know that I think you're basically a pret-ty normal kid? And a great one at that?"

Morgan shrugged in resignation and gave his mother a half-grin. "Yeah, well next time I'm in trouble, I'll remind you."

Laura winked. "That may work for *minor* infractions, young man.

"Let's think about this." She slid her chair next to his. "Maybe...maybe a connection was made between you," she said, nodding toward the jar," and the history of this jar.

He squirmed and clenched his teeth. "I can't tell her about my dreams with the Native American boy," he told himself. "Maybe the stuff about feeling weird is just my imagination?"

A cool breeze wafted through the kitchen as Sara opened the back door.

"Hi," she breathed as she plopped onto a chair seat. "I ran all the way from Jane's house."

She set a cardboard box that once held kitchen matches on the table and slid the cover off.

"Jane thought these arrowheads were so cool," said Sara. A slight frown puckered her brow. "Morgan, could you help me with a better display box?" Crinkling her nose, she added, "This one's kinda dumb. Besides, Daddy said we should keep these nice."

Before Morgan answered, he shot his Mom a look that spoke a silent warning: *Please keep what I told you between us.*

Laura give him a broad smile and winked her understanding.

Morgan relaxed.

He gave Sara a mischievous smile and said, "Sure shrimp

face, as long as you give me a dollar."

In a singsong tone she retorted, "Ha, ha, ha! Sticks and stones may break my bones…" she shrugged a shoulder. "You know the rest, Bro." She reached for a banana. "Besides, I don't have any money, dude."

Plucking an arrowhead from the matchbox, Morgan fingered the serrated edge.

"Say, Mom," he said, "when are we going to the library to do research?

You know, about finding a museum?"

Laura peered at a calendar tacked near the phone. "Hmm, how about this morning?"

"So soon?" Morgan asked, his eyebrows lifting in surprise. "Did you have something else planned?"

He slid the jar closer. "No." He folded his hands around the rounded base, expecting the tingling sensation. But he felt only cold, hard pottery against his skin.

To himself, he wondered, "Are you a magical jar?"

As Laura cleared the table, she thought, "Morgan seems reluctant to give up that jar. If a museum can give us some history surrounding the piece, maybe then it would be easier for him to accept the idea." Studying the kitchen clock, Laura asked, "Can you both be ready in an hour?"

"I can, Mommy," Sara answered cheerfully. She peered into the matchbox where the arrowheads lay on a cushion of milky white cotton. Satisfied they were safe, she slid the cover closed and set the box on a shelf reserved for cookbooks and a collection of coffee mugs.

"Guess so," Morgan muttered as he rose from his chair.

Morgan wandered down the hall to his bedroom and flopped onto the rumpled bed covers. He propped his treasure jar on his chest, hoping for a genie to float from the opening and whisper a message just for him.

ஐ ஐ ஐ

"Buckle up, guys," Laura reminded an hour later as she backed their silver Ford Taurus out of the garage.

ஐ ஐ ஐ

The library housed in a large Victorian, belonged to the Patterson Family until the last heir donated it to the town. The ample grounds were dotted with dogwood trees and scattered native wildflower beds.

The aroma of books in various degrees of age seemed to calm each soul that entered. Miss Clara, the librarian, sat at an ornately carved antique desk. Today she wore a turquoise peasant dress. Wide, white eyelet ruffles around the oval neck helped disguise the snug fit over her plump bodice. Hidden hairpins fastened a bright yellow ribbon around her upswept hairstyle. A cluster of untamed, reddish brown curls sprung from the crown of her head.

She glanced up as they approached and greeted them with a warm, "Good morning." Full lips, glossed with bright pink lipstick, dominated her round face.

Laura answered, "Good morning, Miss Clara."

Sara cast the librarian a timid smile. Her tone hesitant, she asked, "Please ma'am, could you tell us where the Native American history books are?"

A loose curl slipped from the ribbon and jiggled as Miss Clara nodded. She swept a hand toward the back of the room. In her "library voice" she instructed, "Turn left when you get through the archway. On the other side you will see an aisle marked American History."

Morgan turned, looking in the direction, Miss Clara had indicated. "Got it," he said in a low voice. "Oh, I'd like to sign up for computer time today."

"Hmm," said the librarian as she perused the schedule on her desk. "How about two o'clock?"

Morgan glanced at Laura. "Okay, Mom?"

Laura nodded. "Thanks, Miss Clara. That time is perfect." Pointing toward a magazine rack she said, "I'll be over there while you kids browse."

"See you later," said Morgan.

He took the lead through the archway. Seven-foot-tall bookshelves crowded the room. Brass letters spelled various categories at the end of each row.

Morgan stopped and pointed above his head. "Here's the Native American stuff."

"I know," Sara replied in a defensive tone. "I can read."

Morgan grinned. "Yeah, right—till you come to a long word."

"So," said Sara. Glaring at her brother, she thumped a fist against her hip. "Go on. I don't need any help."

Morgan shrugged a shoulder and wandered down the aisle.

Pausing a moment at a section of oversize books, he tipped his head sideways to read the title printed on the narrow spine of one of the books. He pulled it from the shelf and leafed through pages of photographs that captured his interest.

Dark solemn eyes, staring into the camera lens were matched with unsmiling expressions. Groups of Native Americans of various ages, dressed in beaded animal skins, posed beside teepees covered with buffalo hide. Others sat on wooden chairs in front of a small log cabin, built on a treeless prairie.

A faded photograph of four braves mounted on unsaddled horses excited Morgan as he peered at it closely. They sat straight as ramrods, pride etched on their bronze faces, black streaks painted across high cheekbones. Beaded amulets rested against their bare chests. Feathered headdresses trailed down their backs.

"Are those eagle feathers?" Morgan wondered silently. "Maybe these guys were warriors, dressed for battle. That's cool."

He ruffled through several pages, pausing at a photo of a boy about his age. The boy, clad only in buckskin leggings, stood with his moccasin-clad feet slightly apart. He stared over a bow nearly as tall as he, the fingers of both hands curled around the tip. Feather-tipped arrows jutting from a quiver peeked above his shoulder.

Morgan frowned. A faint vision limped at the edge of his memory.

"My dream...He looks like the boy in the canoe, who was with me," thought Morgan.

He lowered his head and raised the book, staring at the boy's features for a long time.

"Get real," he scolded himself. "How could he get into my dream? No way."

He shrugged a shoulder and turned his attention to an elderly man standing beside the boy.

Deep lines furrowed the man's dark-skinned face. Dark eyes glistened from wrinkled pockets. He clutched a buffalo robe that encased his body. Unharnessed long, white hair fanned around his shoulders.

"Gotta have a copy of this picture," Morgan muttered under his breath.

Engrossed in the photo, he was unaware that Sara stood next to him.

"Morgan, did you hear me?" she asked, shoving a book under his nose. "See, I found one. You ready to leave?"

"Dang, you scared me. You're always sneaking up on me."

"Don't have a cow, Morgan," said Sara. She turned her back to him and marched up the aisle.

"Yeah, yeah," said Morgan. He snapped the photograph book shut. "Let's find Mom. I wanna make a copy of a picture before we leave."

Although he really didn't want to, Morgan kept his afternoon appointment at the library for computer time. His lukewarm attempt to locate a museum resulted in failure.

This pleased him.

He reasoned that the treasure jar brought the Native American boy into his dreams. He didn't want to give it to a museum

He wanted to keep it in his room. On a shelf above his pillow.

Chapter Thirteen

Lying in bed that evening, Morgan propped the treasure jar on his chest. The steady pulse in his fingertips throbbed against the cold pottery.

He clamped his eyelids, hoping for sleep. His nighttime dream odysseys with the Native American boy had increased, and had remained his secret.

Morgan knew exactly when the dreams began—at the campground. And he never wanted them to end.

The dream boy called himself Young Eagle.

Several times a night his nighttime playmate tumbled into his dreams, bringing exciting adventures that lurked at the edge of reality. Morgan admired everything about Young Eagle, especially the cool way he looked—the narrow, beaded headband circling his straight black hair, the deerskin loincloth anchored at his waist; that reached just above his knees, and his animal-skin moccasins decorated with beads and small animal bones. The quiver of arrows he carried on his back—totally cool.

Sometimes, during the day, Morgan was sure he caught a

glimpse of Young Eagle in his side vision. But, when he turned his head, it was only an apparition, a mirage, an illusion.

Morgan never spoke of these odd moments to anyone. Secretly, he hoped that Young Eagle actually existed as a human boy somewhere.

One evening at dinner Morgan took a chance and asked, "Are dreams ever, like, maybe pieces of memory of someone you could have known and forgotten?"

Ray reached for his water glass. "Well, I believe they do contain some kind of experience from the past." Frowning slightly, he said, "Why do you ask?"

To prolong an answer, Morgan inspected a green bean speared on his fork. He popped it into his mouth and chewed slowly.

"Well, I've been having awesome dreams of a Native American boy my age," said Morgan. He gave his Dad a wary look before continuing. "He told me his tribe, lived and hunted in the mountains. They fished—what did he call that river? Oh, like…some kind of bird." Morgan frowned into his dinner plate. He shrugged and continued, "And his people—"

"Could I interrupt you a minute, Son?" Ray broke in. "Maybe…" After a moment, he said, "Hawk Valley River? Where you and Sara found the pottery jar and arrowheads?"

"Yeah," said Morgan. "I think that's right." He chewed his mashed potatoes and swallowed. Frowning, he said, "Kinda strange though, you know, that coincidence? Us being in mountains, near a river with that name."

"Well, we had been camping in that area," Laura suggested. "Guess that river's name became part of your dream. But go on, honey. We're listening."

"Okay," said Morgan. "The people survived mostly on

salmon. The men fished from the river with spears. Pretty cool, huh? And get this, he showed me how he hunted game with bow and arrow, big game like deer and elk! And the men prepared for hunting by taking sweat baths. We have adventures in the forest and play games too."

A puzzled expression settled in Morgan's eyes. "Should I tell them?" he wondered. "Oh, jeez, why not."

Morgan took a deep breath and said, "He told me his name was Young Eagle."

Silence.

"*Well, say something!*" cried Morgan. "You're making me nervous."

He released a heavy sigh and licked his lips. "Yeah, I know. I sound goofy."

Sara said, "You ARE goofy, Morgan."

"Don't annoy your brother right now, sweetie," Laura said. She cleared her throat as she set down her coffee cup. "I don't think it sounds goofy at all."

"Okay," said Sara.

"Yeah, Sara. Gimme a break."

Laura smiled and reached for Morgan's hand. Trying to sound normal, but feeling a little anxious, she asked, "So, young man, how long has this been going on?"

Morgan leaned back in his chair. Beaming a broad smile her way, he said, "Ever since I found my treasure—I mean the pottery jar." He glanced around the table. "So you don't think it's too weird?"

Ray smiled. "Hey guy, when I was just about your age, I dreamed of flying. I even flew through windows, and they didn't break." He chuckled at the memory. "Guess I thought I was Superman!" Glancing at Laura, he winked and said, "How about that for weird?" Not expecting a response, he asked, "Do you dream of this Young Eagle often, Son?"

"Yeah, Dad, lots," said Morgan. "I like it when Young Eagle's in my dreams."

Laura didn't know what to think. "I'm a little worried here," she thought, "Now the dream boy interacts with Morgan and he has a NAME?"

Ray didn't know what to make of it either. He decided to take a wait-and-see attitude. He gave his son a confiding wink and teased, "Keep us posted on what you two are up to, okay?"

Morgan issued a thumbs-up gesture. "No prob, Dad. I'll tell Young Eagle 'hello' for you." Lacing his fingers behind his head, he laughed. "Just kidding."

Sara said, "I take it back, Morgan. You're not so goofy. Weird maybe, but you do have cool dreams."

"Thanks, shrimp," said Morgan. "Just for that I won't beat you up later." He glanced sideways at Laura, raising both hands, palms out. "Just kidding, Mom."

Ray shook his head. His quick laugh broke with throaty vibrancy. "Funny boy we have here. Say, anyone up for a picnic at the lake on Saturday?" Folding his arms across his chest, he cautioned, "Don't know about swimming, though. The water may be too cold this late in the season."

"Not that cold," Morgan said. "I can handle it."

"It's okay, Daddy," said Sara. "It'll still be fun."

"Okay, princess," said Ray. He reached over and tousled Sara's curls. Glancing at Laura, he said, "How about it, honey, you up for an afternoon of lounging and feasting?"

Relieved to think of something else, Laura agreed. "Sounds good to me."

❧   ❧   ❧

Sitting on the edge of the bed that evening, Laura asked Ray, "Tell me, was that a true story you told us? You know, the flying dreams?"

Ray grinned. "You bet. Haven't thought of those in years." His eyes held a thoughtful expression as he combed his fingers through his hair, damp from a shower.

"One thing I did notice. Morgan seemed a little apprehensive when he asked about dreams being associated with people he may have known in the past.

"My guess is, maybe that pottery jar he is so fond of could in some way be part of the reason he is dreaming of a Native American boy." He issued a soft chuckle. "Anyway, not to worry, just a lively imagination working."

Laura snuggled the cover around her shoulder. "Maybe you're right." She reached over and switched off her bedside lamp. "It's just that they are recurring, and Morgan describes them like a story. I suppose he could have seen a movie or television program on the subject of Native Americans that prompted one of the characters to enter his dreams. Think that's really possible?"

Plumping a pillow, Ray answered, "Sure. To him, they're exciting adventures. That's all."

But that wasn't all.

There was more. Much, much more.

Chapter Fourteen

Saturday morning Sara, excited about a picnic at the lake, bounded around the kitchen like a rubber ball.

"Could I have an English muffin, please? Mommy, can I wear my new swimsuit?" asked Sara. She sucked a breath. "Oh, let's bring lots of food 'cause I'm going to be super hungry."

Laura leaned against the kitchen counter, arms crossed over her chest.

"Whoa! You are wound up this morning, young lady. Will you please slow down and anchor yourself?"

Raising her arms overhead in a ballet stance, Sara pirouetted across the kitchen floor on her bare feet. She swooped into a chair, pressing her index fingers into her cheeks to suppress her laughter. Her lips turned into a formless bundle.

"See, Mommy," said Sara. "I landed."

Muffins popped from the toaster, plopping on the counter. Laughing, Laura scooped the lightly browned discs onto a plate.

"Okay, funny girl," said Laura. "Now eat your breakfast so we can get this show on the road." She opened the garage door and called, "Breakfast is ready, guys."

"Awesome," Morgan answered. "I'm hungry."

⟨≈⟩   ⟨≈⟩   ⟨≈⟩

Cedar Grove Lake, a popular weekend gathering place, had a good-size dock floating in the middle. The dock served as a diving platform or a place to rest. Acreage above the lake hosted several picnic tables, some sheltered from sun by mature cedar trees. Oaks and aspens curtained the far side of the lake. Leaves tinged with gold hinted that fall was in the air.

Ray backed the van into a vacant parking space. "Aha, there's an empty picnic table waiting for us right over there."

Morgan hopped out of the van. "I'll get these, Dad." He grabbed folded aluminum chairs and propped them against the picnic table.

"Let me know when you guys want lunch," said Laura, spreading a blanket on the grass.

Ray grabbed a pillow and dropped to the blanket. Closing his eyes against the cloudless, indigo sky, he tucked his hands under his head. "Isn't this a great way to spend an afternoon?" he asked.

Easing into a chair, Laura slipped on a bright pink visor and slid sunglasses over her eyes. "Couldn't be better," she answered.

Morgan sat on the picnic bench and toed of his Reeboks and removed his gray T-shirt. He stood and pushed off his jeans, which he wore over dark blue swim trunks.

Pulling off his white athletic socks, balancing on one foot and then the other, he said, "Back in a few," and trotted toward the lake.

Standing on the beach, Morgan cupped his hands against

his forehead, shading his eyes, and searched the dock for anyone he knew. A wide grin spread when he spied Brice, his best
friend, wearing raggedy blue jean cutoffs.

Morgan waved his arms over his head and yelled, "Yo,
Brice. How's the water, dude?"

Brice waved, calling out, "Sweet. But it's kinda cold." He
stood with his hands on his hips, grinning. "Dare you to plunge
in."

Morgan hooted at Brice's challenge. Running full-bore
into shallow water, he dove. A shiver skittered up his back.
"WOW," he shouted.

"Did I hear Morgan?" Ray asked.

"Sounds like he found Brice on the dock," Laura said.

"Good," Ray said, sliding a cap over his face. "They're both
good swimmers. Not to worry."

Laura felt her stomach tense at the "not to worry" part. She
forced herself to relax

*But nothing could stop the impending disaster that lay
ahead.*

As Sara glanced around, she said, "Can I go in the water
now?"

"Sure, honey," said Laura. She dangled inflated, purple water wings from her fingertips. "Don't forget these."

Sara grabbed the water wings and hugged them against her
tummy. "Mommy, do I really need these? I'm not a baby," she
pleaded.

Laura gave Sara a warm smile, and said, "Just for today?"

"Okay," Sara sighed.

They walked hand in hand to the beach. Laura waded into
the water first.

"It's pretty cold," she said. "Sure you want to do this?"

Sara dipped her hands into the water. "It's not THAT cold," she said and struggled into the water wings.

Laura stood in shallow water as Sara kicked and screeched, dog-paddling in circles around her.

After a few minutes Laura said, "Honey, I think it's time to get out. Your lips are burning blue."

"Oh, all right," Sara uttered through chattering teeth.

ᘓᕦᘔ   ᘓᕦᘔ   ᘓᕦᘔ

Morgan reached the dock and settled next to Brice.

Rubbing his arms and shoulders, Morgan said, "The water's not too bad once you're in. You been here long?"

"Not too," said Brice. "We came early 'cause my dad has business stuff later.

"C' mon, race ya across the lake." He pointed. "That big rock, okay?"

"Sure, homey," said Morgan. "But you know I always win."

"Don't bet on it, this time," said Brice.

Toes gripping the edge of the dock, arms in diving position, they counted together: "One, two, three-go!"

Brice finished the race a fraction of a second behind Morgan. Laughing, they smacked each other's dripping palms and crouched on a large slab of granite that slanted into the water.

"Bummer. Close race," Brice relented.

Morgan cuffed his friend's shoulder. "Yeah, right. Let's see who wins the race back."

"Sweet," Brice said as he pushed to his feet. "Let's do it."

"I'm ready," Morgan said. "But be prepared to lose again."

Grinning, Brice said, "Yeah, right."

Morgan paced himself with strong, even strokes. He gained a slight lead until a cramp tightened one leg. Stabbing pain stalled his progress.

Brice reached the dock first and clambered up the ladder. His hands on his knees, he gulped deep breaths. Drops of water flew as he ruffled his hands through his dark brown hair. Breathless, Morgan stumbled up the ladder. He sank to the dock and massaged his aching calf.

"Yeah, yeah," said Morgan. "I know you won." A frown rippled his brow as he straightened his legs, leaned forward and grasped his toes. In a defensive tone he said, "I wasn't far behind you."

Brice slumped to the dock, bundling his arms around his knees. Glancing at his friend he asked, "You okay?"

"Yeah," Morgan said. "Had a cramp. It's gone now." He shot Brice a broad smile. "That's why I didn't beat you."

"Sure, sure," Brice chided. "Better luck next time, homey."

"Right," said Morgan. He turned onto his stomach, folded his arms under his cheek and closed his eyes.

"What if Young Eagle appeared as a real person, like right here, right now?" Morgan thought. "Dang, you are crazy. Get real."

Water thumping against the dock caused a gentle rocking motion, sending Morgan into sleep and a dream.

Young Eagle, his arms outstretched floated toward Morgan.

"Come," said Young Eagle, "let us explore together."

"Great," said Morgan. "Maybe we can find some treasure like my sister and I did on our camping trip."

"Tell me, what treasure did you find?"

"Arrowheads by a river. Here's the best part, we found a small pottery jar."

When Young Eagle didn't respond, Morgan continued.

"When I'm near it, I feel kind of...oh, I don't know...sort of like I'm the same as you in a way. You know, Native American."

He looked away from Young Eagle's dark penetrating eyes. Morgan wondered if what he'd said sounded goofy.

"I believe it right for you to have a Native American name," Young Eagle said. "That would bond us as brothers." A slight frown creased his smooth brow. "I will think on it."

Morgan expelled a long breath, excited by this turn of events. "You mean it? Tell me, how will I pick a name?"

"I shall explain," said Young Eagle. "It is the tradition of my people that at birth we are given a name of an ancestor. I was called Warrior Walking, after my grandfather's father who performed many brave endeavors.

"As a male child, it was tradition, I begin brief vision quests at an early age to strengthen my endurance. When I reached my fourteenth year, I went on an extended vision quest of several days, as is our custom. I journeyed alone, without food, to an isolated place of many spirits known to my people for many, many moons. I denied myself sleep to receive a vision of my guardian animal spirit. Animals appeared and guided me through the ordeal. I performed sacred rituals, denied myself all comfort of clothing and warmth of fire. I prayed, asking Spirit to take pity on me and rescue me from my misery.

"During my vision quest, a bird of prey appeared—I became Young Eagle. From my bird spirit I learned sacred chants, and ritual dances. As in the tradition of my ancestors, I learned to paint symbolic designs on my body. My people believe guardian animal spirits remain with them as long as they live.

"One day the shaman of our village gathered everyone together for a winter spirit dance. That is when I declared, I will be known as Young Eagle.

"At a special ceremony, two arrowheads were prepared especially for me.

"When it was time, I became a hunter of large game. I provided meat, to be shared among the people of my village. Our survival depended upon these animals. Hides from the animals I killed were prepared and tanned for blankets, shelter, clothing and moccasins. Bones were saved to make tools. Nothing of use was discarded."

Morgan sank onto warm grass. He crossed his legs and leaned against a rock.

"Please," said Morgan. "I want to hear more. Tell me about this—what did you call it—vision quest? Why must you do it? Sounds kind of grueling. And, I'm confused. If you were fourteen at the time you went on your vision quest journey…how can you still…wasn't your journey a long time ago?"

A wide smile crinkled Young Eagle's face. His dark eyes sparkled. "These are your dreams. You will materialize whatever illusion you desire. Now it is time to begin your vision quest journey. You will learn your Native American name, from your guardian animal spirit."

"I'm ready," said Morgan. "But how will I go on this journey?"

"It will soon become clear to you. Close your eyes. Your mind must float into timelessness. You will know when the journey must end."

Tingling sensations crawled up Morgan's spine when echoes of distant drumming began and Young Eagle's soft chanting winnowed through his sleeping mind.

The vision quest within the dream had begun.

Chapter Fifteen

*M*organ's heart lurched when he suddenly dropped onto the damp, hard surface of a giant boulder. "Whoa," he said.

He sat up. "I'm in the middle of a lake."

In the gloom, decaying tree trunks coated with dark green moss leaned on boulders or lay partially hidden in brush. A shudder crept up his spine.

"Kinda spooky here," Morgan thought. "I'm cold."

Hugging his knees against his chest, Morgan glanced around. "Is this the sacred place?" he wondered. He swiped a cold hand under his nose. "Will my guardian animal spirit appear?"

Propping his chin on his knees, he rocked back and forth. The low hoot of an owl deep in the forest sounded as lonely as he felt.

"I'm not afraid," Morgan told his dreaming self.

Crackling underbrush and muffled snorts jerked him alert.

"What was that?!" cried Morgan.

Heart pounding, he peered across the water and pushed to his feet.

His hands scrubbing his backside, he whispered, "My butt's numb."

Fear exploded in his chest when a huge brown grizzly bear lumbered out of the forest. The animal sloshed into the lake, water rising around its stubby legs.

Hoping to make himself invisible, Morgan crouched on the rock. He peeked through a crack between his fingers.

The enormous beast scooped out a trout and tossed the quivering fish to the shore. The bear slowly backed out of the water and snuffled its meal.

After a time, the animal raised its massive head sniffing the air. A familiar scent grabbed its attention—human. Round black eyes stared across the water at the image on the rock—Morgan.

The bear slowly nodded its massive head waiting to be recognized. Waiting for the boy to acknowledge this fearless creature as his guardian animal spirit.

In a heartbeat, Morgan instinctually knew he had no reason to be afraid. A flutter of excitement filled his gut at the sudden realization. He sprang to his feet and hurled his hands overhead, punching the air.

"You're my guardian animal spirit, for sure," Morgan cried.

The animal slowly rose up on its hind legs, its brown fur dripping. It's open mouth jutted forward, emitting a long, low roar of approval. It lifted one great paw, as if in greeting.

Morgan returned the gesture.

The bear lowered its bulk and ambled toward the woods. Before disappearing into the gloom, it glanced around, nodding at the boy on the rock.

Morgan whispered, "Good-bye, guardian animal spirit."

Crouching on the rock, Morgan no longer felt lonely. A chant rose in his throat as he performed an ancient Native American tradition, dipping his fingertips into the pond mud, swiping streaks across his forehead and cheekbones. He pushed to his feet, standing tall. Excitement filled his breast as his new name emerged from behind his sleeping eyes.

A message whispered through his dream. "Remember me, your guardian animal spirit. I will live within you as long as I am needed. The name you have chosen is right for you. It will serve you well."

After a dream moment, Young Eagle spoke, "Your journey has ended, my brother."

A ping of joy chased through Morgan's stomach.

"I can't wait to tell you what happened," Morgan said to Young Eagle. His words tumbled into the air. "My guardian animal spirit came, and I visualized my Native American name. Now when we are together I am Standing Bear.

"I have a dream brother!" Morgan excitedly told his sleeping mind.

A serious expression settled in Young Eagle's dark eyes. "Standing Bear is a good name. Your vision quest was successful. Now tell me more about the pottery jar you found."

"Okay," said Morgan. "It's round at the bottom, and curves into a small neck. On the bowl part, if you look real close, you can see something painted."

Morgan fingered the tip of an arrow.

"Please, Standing Bear, continue," said Young Eagle.

"This is gonna sound weird, but sometimes when I hold it, I feel kinda—" he drew a deep breath, releasing it slowly—"sad."

Young Eagle's eyes turned somber. "My brother, Standing Bear, I believe you unearthed a burial urn. A Spirit Jar."

"A Spirit Jar?" asked Morgan.

"I shall explain, said Young Eagle. When my people pass into the spirit world, cremation is part of our burial ceremony. Ashes are stored in a vessel, such as you describe, then buried in sacred ground. That is why you feel sadness when you hold it. Even though the ashes have vanished, the spirit remains in the jar and the ground where you found it. My brother, the Spirit Jar must be returned."

A spear of pain burst through Morgan's chest. He drew a shuddering breath. "No way. You know that for sure?"

Young Eagle's image began to fade.

Morgan struggled to stay in the dream. "Wait!" he called after Young Eagle, "don't go."

But his questions were smothered in his aching throat, leaving a heavy heart within the dream.

༺༻   ༺༻   ༺༻

"Hey, dude, wake up," Brice said, nudging Morgan with a bare foot. "Chill. You were moaning. Must've been having a nightmare."

Shielding his eyes from the sun, Morgan peeked through his splayed fingers. He rolled onto his side away from Brice. He fingered the single claw of a grizzly bear fastened on a leather strand around his neck, a memento purchased at Mr. Harold's store.

The smooth, curved totem felt like it belonged close to his heart.

"Guess I fell asleep," Morgan murmured.

Brice pushed to his feet. Bending forward he touched the dock with his fingertips. "Race you to that rock again. Dollar says you can't beat me."

Struggling to his feet, Morgan said, "Yeah, right."

Posed in diving positions, they looked at one another and grinned. As they sprang from the dock, "Geronimo!" rang over the lake.

Halfway to the rock, Morgan felt intense shooting pain in his leg again.

Panic seared through him as he fought to keep his head above water.

"Brice," he sputtered through a mouthful of water.

But his friend did not hear his weak cry for help.

Morgan's fatigued arms failed to keep him afloat. His ears roared as he sank into the lake.

Then everything went black.

Chapter Sixteen

Ray stood on the sandy beach, observing the boys as they swam away from the dock.

"Wait a minute," he said, frowning into the glaring sun. "Did Morgan slow down?"

Alarmed by a sense that Morgan could be in trouble, he sprinted into shallow water, shouting, "HANG ON, SON. I'M COMING."

His heart sank when he saw Morgan disappear from the surface of the lake.

Brice scampered onto the slippery surface of the granite rock. Through short breaths from exertion, he declared, "Hey, dude. I told you I'd win."

No response.

"Hey, guy," he said. "Where the heck are you?" He frowned, eyes skating over the rippling surface.

His heart tightened with fear at what he saw—Morgan's head burst from the water, his arms thrashing.

Brice sensing something was terribly wrong, leaped up and down, frantically waving, yelling "HELP! HELP! MY

FRIEND IS IN TROUBLE."

Brice took a deep breath and dove. A few yards from the dock, treading water, he searched the surface. Morgan was nowhere in sight. Heart pounding, he swam to the dock and grabbed the wooden ladder. His legs quivered as he climbed onto the bottom rung. He stifled a sob when he saw Ray propelling through the water, foam boiling in his wake.

"Over there, Mr. Shephard," cried Brice. "I think that's where I last saw him."

Below the surface of the lake, golden light bubbled around Morgan.

Tingling sensations enveloped his body. His mind floated in unmeasured time.

"Am I drowning," Morgan wondered.

An image of the bear, his guardian animal spirit, emerged behind his closed eyes, calming his fear.

Exhausted, Morgan surrendered.

Suddenly, Young Eagle's voice penetrated his drowsy trance.

"I am here also, Standing Bear."

Morgan slowly opened his heavy eyelids, but he could not see.

Darkness surrounded him.

"Do not fear," said Young Eagle. "All is as it should be." He grasped Morgan's hand and pulled him from the water. "We must take a journey together. I have something to show you."

The wind rumbled, sweeping Morgan upward. It whipped him upside down, pitching his stomach into a somersault. He sucked air, swallowed.

Morgan thought: "Going to puke…I'm doomed…help…"

Then he heard Young Eagle whisper, "You are safe, Standing

Bear."

Calm settled into Morgan's lurching heart. Slowly, slowly he descended into a void of darkness, straining to see, but still sightless.

Sleep and a dream engulfed his weary mind..

Plunk!

Landing on a firm surface, Morgan staggered. "Dirt—it's dirt," he said in an excited dream voice.

Grass brushed his bare legs. He cocked his head, listening to the forest speaking. Branches creaked as breezes stirred the air. Water splashing over river rocks sprayed his body. A leaf, surrendering to winter, settled onto his outstretched palm.

Young Eagle grasped Morgan's elbow and guided him over the rocky terrain.

In a tentative tone, Morgan asked, "Tell me, where are you taking me?"

Suddenly, a choral chant pierced the forest. Thundering drumbeats slammed his chest. Fire scorched his outstretched hands. Smoke stung his unseeing eyes. A putrid scent invaded his unconscious mind. Death?

Swiping a tear sliding down his cheek, Morgan said, "This is a cremation ceremony."

"Yes," replied Young Eagle. "You are witnessing an ancient sacred tradition.

"It is the way of my people."

These words came into Morgan's unconscious mind, as if through thick cotton.

Morgan sensed he was now alone.

The dream faded.

But he knew what this journey was about.

And what he must do.

Morgan made a silent promise to Young Eagle.

Chapter Seventeen

Laura sat on the picnic bench, tossing peanuts to hungry birds. She watched two blue jays squawking and battling over one nut. Flinging a handful to the bossy feathered creatures, she said, "I'd like a soft drink. Would you like one, Sara?"

"Thanks, Mommy."

Sara hummed as she sat at the picnic table, filling in pictures of animals with bright-colored markers.

"There's a small crowd gathered on the beach," Laura said. "Wonder what's going on?"

"Mommy, is something wrong?"

"I don't know," Laura said, squeezing Sara's hand. "Someone may be ill. I think I saw your daddy swimming toward the dock."

"C'mon," said Laura. "Let's go see. Maybe we can help."

At the edge of the lake, Laura looked for Morgan. Under her breath she said, "Last time I saw him, he and Brice were on the dock."

Laura's hand trembled as she tugged at the brim of her visor. Through the glare of sun-spiked water, she strained to see what was happening.

She felt her stomach tighten. A voice at the back of her head whispered, "Morgan's in trouble."

"No," Laura protested, "he...he's with Brice."

Sara pointed toward the water. "Mommy, look. There's Daddy."

Icicles of fear jabbed the space below her heart. She knew that Morgan was somewhere under the surface and needed help *now.*

Ray reached the area where Brice pointed. He plunged, warning himself not to panic. His vision cloudy in the murky water, he swam in tight circles, arms plowing through fluid that felt thick as molasses. His lungs begging for air, he pushed to the surface and breathed deeply. Not wasting a moment, he jackknifed into the water.

Ray saw Morgan's limp body a few feet ahead. Streams of dot-size air bubbles drifted from his nose. He reached for the boy and, with one arm hugging his torso, kicked to the surface.

Laura's throat contracted when she saw Ray surface with a body. Instinctively, she knew, "Oh, Morgan," she moaned.

Someone in the crowd said, "We called the paramedics. They'll be here in a few minutes."

Carol, Brice's mother, asked, "Laura, would you like me to get Sara away from the beach?"

Laura shivered and nodded. She crouched in front of Sara and said, "Honey, I think it best you go with Carol and wait for me."

Choked with fear, Sara nodded. Tears streamed over her cheeks as she trudged up the hill. She sank to the grass and folded her trembling arms around her knees. Carol sat beside her and circled an arm around the child's shoulders.

Laura sloshed through shallow water toward Ray. Tears burned her eyes as she stroked her son's pale cheek. "Oh, Ray…is he…is he?"

Ambulance sirens wailed in the distance as Ray carried Morgan up the sandy beach. A hint of his son's warm breath against his cheek gave him hope.

"He's unconscious," Ray said to Laura.

A woman spread a blanket across the grass and said, "Here, put the boy on this." Ray laid Morgan on his side.

Laura dropped to her knees and clutched Morgan's pale hand. She began massaging, blowing warm breath onto his cold flesh. Swallowing unshed tears, she pleaded quietly, "Please, God. Send us your gentle mercy."

A moment later, flashing red lights appeared. Doors flew open as the stark white vehicle halted next to the inert boy. A two-person paramedic team exited quickly.

A male paramedic knelt beside Morgan and gently tilted his head. Using a tongue depressor, he checked for debris clogging the throat. "It's clear," he said.

Crouching beside Morgan, a female paramedic opened a black leather medical bag. She positioned a stethoscope on his chest and back. "How long was he underwater?" she asked.

Ray choked, "I… I don't know for sure. Maybe two, three minutes."

She nodded, concern shadowing her eyes. After what seemed an eternity, she said, "There it is. Weak, but beating steady."

Morgan coughed and choked as lake water flowed from his open mouth.

"Okay, son," said the woman paramedic. "Take it easy.

You're doing fine. Your family's right here."

The small crowd issued a unanimous, "All right!"

Sara stood beside Carol, her slight body shivering.

Carol whispered, "Go to your family, honey. Everything's okay."

Laura reached out and gathered Sara in her arms. "Your brother is going to be fine, sweetie." She kissed her flushed cheek. "He gave us quite a scare, huh?"

Ray reassured Sara with a wink and a broad smile. He glanced at the names stitched in red across the pockets of the paramedics, white shirts. "Cheryl and Steve, is it?"

They nodded a serious affirmative.

"Thank you for bringing him back to us," said Ray.

Steve answered for them both. "You're welcome. Glad we got here in time." He pulled a stretcher from the rear opening of the ambulance and pressed a lever, turning it into a rolling gurney.

Still checking vital signs, Cheryl squeezed Morgan's hand. Giving him a reassuring smile, she said, "Doing great, young man." She adjusted the blanket over him and added, "Don't try to talk just yet."

Cheryl stood, reached into a shirt pocket, and plucked out a ballpoint pen. A sympathetic expression crossed her face. "I need to ask a couple of questions," she said to Ray. "They'll get the rest of the information at the hospital."

"Sure thing," Ray answered softly. He swept his icy hands over his large biceps, which begged for warmth. Someone in the crowd handed him a towel.

Steve pulled off his thin latex gloves and poked them into a pocket.

The paramedics each gripped a corner of the blanket and

swung Morgan onto the chrome gurney. Steve winked at Morgan. "You're going for a ride in an ambulance, young man."

Laura glanced at Steve as she brushed damp hair from her son's forehead. "Please, may I ride with him?"

"Of course, ma' am. No problem."

Ray squeezed Laura's hand. "I'll just grab a shirt. We'll meet you at the hospital."

Brice sagged against the open door of the ambulance, a towel draped over his hunched shoulders. As the paramedics slid the stretcher in, he said, "I'm sorry, Morgan, that I wasn't there to help you." His eyes filled with tears as he felt Laura's embrace.

"It's okay, Brice," said Laura. "It's not your fault."

Curious about the inside of an ambulance, Morgan peered over the edge of the blanket tucked under his chin. Shiny chrome equipment lined the wall of the van like miniature robots.

"Hope they're not going to use all this stuff on me," he thought.

In spite of his terrifying experience, Morgan looked forward to the ride.

"Bet none of the guys ever rode in an ambulance." Morgan mused to himself. "Wait until I tell 'em about all the stuff packed in here."

Chapter Eighteen

The faint smell of disinfectant alcohol and other undefined medication aromas permeated the air in the emergency room. A female attendant approached, clad in a deep pink smock, clutching a metal clipboard to her chest. She smiled, gesturing toward a row of white plastic chairs and said, "You folks can wait there."

"Thank you," Laura said.

"I'll stay with Morgan," Ray said. "You and Sara be okay?"

Laura nodded, tapping the form-layered clipboard with a ball point pen. "I have plenty to keep me busy."

They shared a smile. "Yeah," said Ray. "There's always paperwork." He turned and followed the paramedics into an examination cubicle.

The resident doctor appeared and extended a hand to Ray, issuing a firm handshake. "Mr. Shephard, I'm Dr. Holly Jenkins." She leaned over the gurney. "So, what's going on with you, young man? Morgan is it?"

Morgan nodded and said, "I'm okay now." Her fingers felt warm as she tapped his chest and asked him to breathe deep.

"Had a cramp in my leg. I couldn't swim."

"Oh, in the calf area?" asked the doctor.

"Yeah, my left leg," Morgan said, "but it's good now."

Dr. Jenkins smiled. "Well, let's check you out anyway." She palpated the leg. "Any pain here?"

"No, ma' am."

Over her reading glasses, the doctor smiled at Ray and jotted a note in the chart. "Let your pediatrician know about the cramp. But I would like to get a chest X-ray."

A worried look passed between Morgan and Ray.

"I just want to make sure the lungs are clear," said Dr. Jenkins.

A male X-ray technician joined the doctor. Gold flecks glinted in his chocolate brown eyes when he smiled. "My name's Anthony," he said in a friendly tone. "How are you doing, Morgan?"

Morgan pulled the blanket to his chin. "Fine...I guess. Never had an X-ray before though."

Anthony gave Morgan a two-thumbs up. "Won't hurt a bit, son." Rolling the gurney down the wide hall, he added, "Easy as taking your picture."

About an hour later, Dr. Jenkins bustled through a swinging door. A smile split her round face as she approached the waiting family.

"The X-ray shows his lungs are clear," she announced. "Get him to your pediatrician ASAP for a follow-up examination."

Ray heaved a sigh of relief as he reached for Laura. "Our boy is going to be okay," he said, kissing her flushed cheek.

"They parted and turned toward the doctor. "Thank you very much, Dr. Jenkins. I'll make an appointment early Monday," Laura said.

"You're very welcome," said the doctor. She slid a hand into a pocket of her blue smock and handed a business card to Laura. "Morgan is resting in room 104. You can take him home in a while." She turned and hurried toward a nurse calling for assistance. "You can reach me anytime," she called over her shoulder.

Near the door of Room 104, the drone from a motorized hospital bed strayed into the hallway.

As the family entered the room, Morgan grinned sheepishly. "Just testing the controls."

"Let me see," said Sara, climbing onto the bed.

"Don't wear it out, shrimp," said Morgan, handing her the remote. He turned on his side and adjusted the blanket around his body. "That ambulance ride was cool."

Laura pulled a chair next to the bed and reached for his hand. "Dr. Jenkins said we can take you home after you have rested a bit."

Ray leaned against the wall behind Laura's chair. He folded his arms across his chest. "Leg cramp, huh?" he said without expecting an explanation. "Well, that's enough to cause big trouble in the water."

Laura pressed her cheek against Morgan's warm hand. The steady pulse beating in his wrist reassured her. He's alive!

Morgan slept uninterrupted until his parents' whispers roused him. He kept his eyes closed and burrowed under the covers, recalling his dream journey with Young Eagle to a sacred cremation ceremony.

Shivering under the warmth of the blanket, Morgan told himself, "I didn't disturb sacred ground on purpose. And I will return the Spirit Jar."

Dragging a pillow from under his head, he clutched it

against his chest and drew a shuddering breath. Shoving his face into the pillow, he muffled a groan as he thought, "Don't know how though."

"This…this situation is totally out of control," he told himself.

Laura rose from her chair. "Are you okay, sweetie? I thought I heard you moaning."

"He may be reliving the day," Ray answered quietly. His eyes narrowed. "Hope he doesn't have nightmares over this. Didn't think to ask Dr. Jenkins about sleep disturbances."

"We'll talk to the doctor about that before we leave," Laura said in a low tone.

Sara climbed onto the foot of the bed. "Morgan's awake. Can we go home now?"

Morgan flipped back the blanket and frowned at the ceiling.

Tossing gray sweat pants and a black, paint-stained T-shirt onto the bed, Ray said, "We didn't bring your clothes. But I found these in the van. They're somewhat dusty, but they'll do." He laid some plastic flip-flops on the floor. "Get dressed and we're out of here."

Ushering Sara from the room, Laura said, "I'll find Dr. Jenkins and ask her if there's anything we should watch for." She looked over her shoulder at Ray, mouthing a silent, "You know."

Ray winked understanding. "We'll meet you in the lobby." Massaging an earlobe, he turned toward Morgan and said, "I'll be in the hall. Call if you need me."

"Okay," Morgan answered. He yanked the sweats under the sheet. "Be there in a minute." He screwed his expression into a frown, tugging the waistband over his hips. He flipped the sheet aside, scooted to the edge of the bed, and shrugged into the T-shirt. A double sneeze from the dusty clothes watered his eyes.

He sat on the edge of the bed thinking, "I was so scared today. My arms…so tired…couldn't keep my head above water." Shivers raced up his spine. "*I was drowning.*"

Abruptly, Morgan's stomach rolled over. Bile boiled at the back of his throat.

"*OhmiGod!*" he moaned. "The cremation ceremony—my promise to Young Eagle. How can I keep it?" Morgan said under his breath.

Swallowing again, and again to keep from vomiting, he dashed through the bathroom door and braced his hands on top of the toilet tank. After a minute of deep breathing he felt better. Almost normal.

From the doorway, Ray asked, "Are you okay, Son?"

"I'm okay now," Morgan answered, easing upright, wobbling slightly.

"Jeez, that was stupid," he thought as he gulped water from a plastic cup.

Morgan clutched his bear claw pendant. Sliding his thumb over the smooth curved surface, he stared at the claw hoping to receive a message. A solution to his dilemma.

No helpful plan leaped into his thoughts.

Morgan was on his own.

Chapter Nineteen

The back porch door creaked as Laura pulled it open. She glanced at the cooler where Carol had offered to leave it.

"We'll have our picnic tonight," she thought. To Morgan, she said, "Why don't you get into your pj's. You can rest on the couch. I'll get a plate of food for you and Sara. You guys can eat at the coffee table."

"Okay, Mom," Morgan said.

After dinner, Laura and Ray lingered over a nightcap of hot, spicy herb tea. A Tiffany-glass lamp above the table cast soft light over their tired expressions.

Laura inhaled fragrant steam and, as if by magic, the grave situation of the afternoon melted. She reached across the table and clasped Ray's hand. Tears glistened her eyes. "When I saw you carrying Morgan, I was terrified. He looked so small in your arms."

Ray's raspy voice caught in his throat. "This afternoon is history, my love. He's safe."

Sara wandered into the kitchen. She stretched and hopped onto her father's lap. "Morgan's sleeping. He didn't even finish all his dinner." The hint of a frown nudged her brow as she plucked imaginary lint from her father's T-shirt and asked, "Mommy, do I have to go to school Monday?"

"Yes, missy, you must," said Laura. "I don't know about your brother. It depends on what Dr. Matthews recommends. He may want Morgan to stay home and rest a couple of days."

Ray hugged Sara. "You know what, princess? I think it is time for bed. This has been one hell of a day!"

Sara elbowed him in the ribs. "*Daddy!*" You said a naughty word."

"I know, I know, you caught me," said Ray. He kissed her cheek. "But you must admit, it has been an exhausting day."

Nodding her head slowly in agreement, Laura rose and walked into the living room. Morgan was curled on the couch. His hands stacked under his cheek. She reached down and gently shook his shoulder. "Time to go to bed," she said quietly.

Half asleep, Morgan shuffled to his room and dropped into bed. Laura tucked the comforter around him. She felt his forehead, found it cool. Satisfied that danger had passed, she left him snoring softly.

☙ ☙ ☙

Sunday morning, dusky clouds boiled over the eastern hills. Misty rain chilled the air.

Morgan huddled under his rumpled covers, only his head sticking out like a turtle. He stared at a mist-beaded windowpane thinking, "Just like I feel—gray."

Anxiety crawled through him as the same nagging question radiated through his mind—how was he going to return the

Spirit Jar?

Morgan bit his lower lip. "Can't stand this. This worry stuff is a total bummer," he murmured and yanked the comforter over his head. He craved sleep.

"Maybe," Morgan thought, "I'll have a great dream with Young Eagle, and, when I wake up, everything will be solved. No problem."

But Morgan knew otherwise. "Dream on," he mumbled out loud.

Chapter Twenty

Monday morning Ray left for work. Sara caught the bus for school. Morgan had a doctor's appointment.

The autumn sun streamed through the kitchen window. A cardinal swooped to the backyard feeder, chirping a morning greeting.

Laura smiled, musing to herself, "What a difference from yesterday's gloom."

The sound of bare feet padding down the hall drew her attention. Morgan shuffled into the room and slumped to a chair. He leaned over and rested his head on an outstretched arm.

"Guess I'm still tired," he said.

"Good morning," said Laura. "How about some breakfast? That should perk you up." She ruffled his hair. "He's not himself," she thought.

Morgan yawned. "Yeah, sounds okay, Mom." He sat up as she set a giant glass of orange juice down. After a sip he asked, "Mom, do I have to go to the doctor? I feel good. Honest."

Turning from the stove, she said, "Sorry, no choice in this matter." Placing a plate of steaming scrambled eggs before him, she said, "Here you go. This will make you feel even better."

Elongating his response, he moaned, "All riiight." Dipping a fork into his breakfast, he puffed a resigned sigh.

"We don't have much time," Laura said, buttering a piece of toast, "before we have to leave for Dr. Matthew's office."

Morgan finished eating and slowly rose from his chair, saying, "Okay…I just want to…" He shrugged a shoulder and left the room.

Laura stared at his back. "That kid," she thought to herself. Concern veiled her eyes. "He's hiding something."

She waited a few minutes before following him. His bedroom door was open. As she leaned against the doorjamb, her eyes softened at the sight.

Morgan lay on his side, his arms curled around the pottery jar—his treasure jar.

Sensing her presence, he squeezed his eyes tight, to dam the tears threatening to spill. He had hoped that if he kept the treasure jar close, he would think of a solution to his dilemma. But that didn't happen.

"Time to get dressed," Laura said.

"I know, Mom."

"Meet you in the kitchen when you're ready."

Arguments with himself over his problem resulted in a headache. "I can't just jump in the van and take off for the mountains by myself," Morgan told himself. "Dang, I don't know how to drive yet. Anyway, I'd probably get lost."

Morgan's shoulders sagged as he sat on the edge of the bed. A long groan filled the small room as he tucked his head between his hands and rocked slightly forward and back, trying to ease the pain of the distressing situation facing him.

"Are you almost ready?" his mom called from the kitchen.

"Just about," answered Morgan.

He pushed to his feet, pulled on his blue jeans, and struggled into a clean T-shirt. Under his breath he said, "My major problem is, how am I going to explain to Mom and Dad why I have to return to the campground." Shaking his head slowly, he added, "Maybe they'll think I'm crazy or not even believe my story about the journey with Young Eagle to the cremation ceremony."

As he reached for the doorknob, Morgan froze.

Goose bumps prickled his scalp. He peered at the photograph of the Native American boy tacked to the back of his bedroom door.

The boy and his elderly companion seemed to be staring directly at him. Their dark, solemn eyes followed him, as he moved a few inches left then right, of the picture.

Morgan leaned closer, "Something's weird," he said. "But…"

His mom's voice broke into his concentration, "Morgan, I'm waiting."

"Okay, Mom," he called out.

Morgan smoothed a hand over the picture, a puzzled expression veiled his eyes.

Hearing his mom backing the car out of the garage, he closed his bedroom door and hurried out of the house.

꽃   꽃   꽃

Morgan's checkup consisted of the usual.

After Dr. Matthews tucked his stethoscope into a pocket of his white smock, he said in a positive tone, "Young man, you survived your accident very well." A broad smile traveled to his hazel eyes. "Can't find a thing wrong. How do you feel about that?"

Naked to the waist, Morgan, sat on the edge of the examination table, staring at the white tile floor. He looked up and gave the doctor a faint smile. "I feel okay, Dr. Matthews." He shrugged. "I told Mom and Dad I was fine."

The crisp white paper covering the padded table crinkled as Morgan stepped to the floor.

Morgan just wanted to get out of there. He felt he'd had enough doctoring lately. Managing a normal tone, he asked, "Mom, can we go now?"

"In a minute," Laura said. She turned toward the doctor. "So the leg cramp isn't anything to worry about?" She hesitated. "Growing pains?"

Dr. Matthews glanced at notes from a medical file. "He's an inch taller than when I last saw him. A heating pad could help. And, of course, a multivitamin every day. Potassium-enriched foods are also helpful, like bananas, OJ, and potatoes." He chuckled and looked at Morgan over his reading glasses. "You're going to be tall, young man."

"Thanks," Morgan said, slouching against the examination table. "So big deal," he thought, buttoning his shirt. "I've got a lot more on my mind besides my height." At the door he turned and said, "I'm going to the waiting room, Mom."

After Morgan had closed the door, Laura said, "Sorry if he seemed distant. He's...I don't know. Maybe it's his age."

Dr. Matthews adjusted his glasses, clearing his throat. "Don't worry. He's doing fine. By the way, how's Sara doing?"

"Oh, Sara's being Sara," Laura answered, her tone light. "I believe she's scheduled for a checkup next month."

"I'll see you then," the doctor answered and escorted her to the reception desk.

As they hurried from the doctor's office, Laura circled an arm around Morgan's shoulders, she pressed a quick hug. "How about a celebration? I'll treat you to lunch at Emily's Place." She unlocked the car door to let him in. As she slid behind the steering wheel, she mused in silence, "A little bribery doesn't hurt. Maybe he'll fess up and tell me what's bothering him."

Morgan slouched against the door, the seat belt straining against his chest. He stared out the side window. "Don't feel much like a party," he said. He glanced sideways at his Mom, giving her a half-smile. "Sorry. Don't mean to be such a pain. Just don't wanna talk right now." He drew a deep breath. "Guess I could eat something, though."

"Great, I'm starved." Laura glanced over at him. "Hey, you okay? Kinda cranky? Dr. Matthews said you were fine."

"Yeah, I know, Mom," said Morgan. "Just thinking about something."

He couldn't erase the argument that continued in his head: "It's no big deal. Just talk to them. They'll understand when you explain everything. They love you. Huh! Well, maybe not so much today." He grinned at his silent joke.

Morgan reached toward the radio and dialed to his favorite rock station. Snapping his fingers to the beat of one of his favorite songs, he said, "Let's eat."

Laura shook her head and said, "Well, so nice to have a cheerful date for lunch."

Morgan knew there was no way he could avoid what needed to be done—return to the campground with the Spirit Jar.

He just didn't know how to make it happen.

Desperate, Morgan needed a plan.

Chapter Twenty-one

Laura sipped her coffee, watching Morgan fiddle with the wrapper from his straw, her thoughts wandering. "These dreams…what are they really about?" she asked herself. Her intuition whispered, "Something about that treasure jar. Lately, Morgan seems to be hiding behind an invisible wall. Ever since we got home from vacation, there are moments…"

Morgan frowned into his lap. "Can't finish this sandwich, Mom." He gave her a wan smile. "I thought I was hungry."

"Sweetheart, are you sure there's nothing you want to talk about?" asked Laura. She reached over and squeezed his forearm.

Through a heavy sigh, Morgan said, "No. Not really."

Thinking another approach may help her son open up, Laura asked, "By the way, have you been having more dreams with Young Eagle?"

"Yeah," he answered. "A couple."

Laura waited for Morgan to continue.

Silence.

Morgan rose from his chair. "Can we go now?"

"Okay," sighed Laura.

Digging in her purse for her wallet she thought, "He's sure not going to tell me what's up with him."

Once home, Laura phoned Ray and reported that Dr. Matthews had found everything physically normal. Morgan could return to school the next day. She hung up the phone, longing for a comforting cup of herb tea.

Waiting for water to heat, she leaned against the kitchen counter and gazed at Morgan slouched in a chair, his expression troubled.

Laura didn't know how she could unlock Morgan's silence. His unwillingness to confide in her.

"Patience," she told herself. "It'll work out."

After a few minutes, without a word, Morgan rose from the chair, and wandered out of the kitchen.

In his room, he flopped onto the bed and rolled a pillow over his head. Soon, drowsiness lured him into sleep, the blizzard of confused thoughts fading.

Dream-fog swirled around his bare legs. Morgan fingered the soft animal skin that surrounded his waist, peering at an approaching figure, veiled by mist.

It was Young Eagle.

Happiness bubbled in Morgan's chest as he called out in his dream voice, "I've missed you, my brother. Can you stay?"

"I am here for now, Standing Bear," said Young Eagle. A wide smile spread into his eyes. "I wanted to appear earlier but could not."

"Can we have an adventure?" asked Morgan.

Young Eagle pulled a bow from the quiver hanging down his back.

"Standing Bear, do you remember our journey where I revealed to you the history of my people's burial custom?"

Morgan attached an arrow to his bow and aimed at an invisible target. "Sure, I remember."

Silence spilled between them. Young Eagle stared at Morgan, offering his dream brother an unspoken message: "When it is time, Standing Bear, the final truth of the Spirit Jar will become known to you."

"Show me a place where you find adventure," *Morgan begged. He began to run. He called over his shoulder,* "C'mon, Young Eagle. Let's have fun."

"Follow me, Standing Bear, to the river."

Echoes of laughter vibrated through the dream as they plunged into rapid moving water. They bodysurfed downstream, tumbling over a waterfall.

Submerged, Morgan gagged.

His chest heaved.

Numb with fear, boiling in his gut, he sank into darkness.

A familiar voice penetrated his consciousness: "Morgan, Morgan, wake up."

Rousing from sleep, momentarily disoriented, Morgan blinked to clear his blurred vision, "Dad?" Confused, he said, "I'm in my own room." He turned his head toward the wall, thinking, "What a nightmare ending to *that* one."

Ray, sitting on the edge of the bed, said, "It's okay, Son." A worried expression veiled his eyes. "You seemed agitated for a moment. Bad dream?"

Morgan yawned, avoiding an answer. He stretched his arms

over his head. "Just bizarre." His eyes tinted with caution, he added, "The Native American boy and I...we were having fun until..." He shrugged. "Ah, everything just turned weird, that's all."

"Sure you don't want to talk about it?" Ray asked as he rose from the bed.

He waited in the doorway.

"No, Dad. Maybe later. Would you close the door, please?"

The photograph of the Native American boy and his elderly companion trembled.

Morgan's eyes glazed.

Gradually the photograph enlarged and floated from the door, toward him. He sat up and staggered across the room.

"What the heck's going on?" he said, careful to keep his voice low. The photograph wavered in midair a moment then swooped to the door, where he had tacked it.

Scrubbing his eyelids, Morgan whispered, "Whoa! I didn't see that. Did I?"

He warily touched the photograph with his fingertips.

Morgan placed his thumb on the tack and pressed hard to make sure it was fastened tight.

It was.

He backed up to his desk and reached behind, groping for a magnifying glass. Frowning, he peered through the lens, isolating the features of the young face.

His stomach tumbled. He knew—without a doubt—it was Young Eagle.

"So," he said quietly, "you were real, a long time ago. *A real human boy!*"

Morgan drew a deep breath, releasing it slowly.

"I better find a good time to explain some things," he said.

"And ask for help.

Like—soon."

Ray waited in the hallway, taking a minute to think. It concerned him that Morgan spoke of this dream boy as if he were a friend from school. "Should we be concerned about his obvious attachment to this illusionary boy?" he silently wondered. He sighed, thumbing his chin. "He was definitely agitated before I woke him. Nightmare? Probably."

When Morgan emerged from his room, he was surprised to see his dad.

"Hey, waiting for me?" he asked.

"Hey, yourself," said Ray. He draped an arm around Morgan's shoulders. "You know, Son, our dreaming mind can create such vivid scenes—almost real." He hesitated. "This boy…Young Eagle. Well, I would think because you like being with him, that's probably why you dream of him often. Does that make sense to you?"

Misery stained Morgan's expression. Staring at the carpet, he wondered silently, "How can I tell Dad, that Young Eagle's picture is tacked to my bedroom door!?"

"I need help, before I go crazy."

He gave his dad a wan smile, "Guess it does. Sort of."

Ray gently lifted Morgan's chin and looked into his eyes. "If you have something you want to tell us, Mom and I are here." He jammed his hands into his chino pants pockets. "I have an idea. You could write about your dreams, like in a journal. What do you think?"

Morgan looked askance at Ray. A hint of a smile tugged at the corner of his mouth. In a confiding tone, he said, "Dad, a diary like the one Grandma gave Sara for her birthday? She keeps it hidden, you know, in her room." He snickered.

"Kinda stupid where she put it—under her mattress."

Ray issued a soft chuckle. "Well, I hope you respect her privacy. That diary is her private world. She needs to feel safe to express her thoughts." He reached over and squeezed the back of Morgan's neck. "A journal is different. It would be a detailed record, like in your case, of your dream adventures with Young Eagle. Will you give the idea some thought?"

"Sure, Dad."

"Good. Let's eat. We'll talk about the journal idea later."

"Wish it were that simple," Morgan thought silently. "How do I explain to Mom and Dad that Young Eagle is pinned to my bedroom door?"

He puffed a long sigh. *I mean a picture of him! This is getting outrageously complicated!*

Chapter Twenty-two

"Dinner's ready," Laura announced from the kitchen. She placed a chilled green salad on the table.

Morgan's bleak expression, as he entered the room and sank to a chair, predicted something amiss.

"What's up?" asked Laura.

A slight shake of Ray's head froze further questions. He reached over and squeezed Laura's hand.

Morgan's instinct told him the moment had arrived. Time to confess his gigantic dilemma. He wanted, finally, to rid himself of the turmoil blazing through his mind.

Sara scooted onto a chair. Her gaze flickered over unsmiling faces around the table. "What's wrong?" she asked.

"Nothing serious, honey," Laura said. "I think your brother has something he wants to talk about." She sank to a chair next to Morgan. "Sweetie, we feel something has been troubling you the past few days. Please, talk to us."

"You can trust us to listen, Morgan," said Ray. "We'll give our best shot to understand anything you want to talk about. In fact, you can count on it."

Morgan expelled a long breath. "I know, Dad. I'm just not sure how to start."

"At the beginning," said Ray.

"Okay," Morgan said, "here goes."

Licking his dry lips, Morgan began. "Well, Young Eagle reminded me about something I need to do for him."

Unsure how his parents would react, he concentrated on polishing a spoon with a paper napkin.

"Anyway," Morgan continued, "I've been kinda mixed-up lately. I have a big problem." Raising his eyes toward the ceiling he said, "I mean BIG."

Sara stared, wide-eyed. Her head swiveled back and forth from Ray to Laura. Scared that her brother was going to cry, she handed him a napkin. Not sure what else to do, she said, "Hey, Morgan. Daddy says whatever it is, it's okay."

Morgan gave her a wan smile. "Oh, Sis, you just don't *know*." He leaned back in his chair. After a moment he said, "Sara, would you go to my room and get the treasure jar?"

Eager to help, she quickly brought the jar and set it in front of Morgan.

He stared at the precious object a moment. He brushed his sweaty palms over his thighs, leaving damp smudges on his jeans.

"Go ahead, sweetie, don't stop," Laura coaxed. "We'll just sit here and listen."

"I...I...have to do something," Morgan began. He paused, twisting his mouth. "Like go somewhere that's pretty far away."

He waited for reactions, but his parents remained quiet.

In a hesitant tone, he continued, "I took something away from a place—actually a sacred place." He rushed on, before he lost his nerve. "It wasn't okay for me…" he stared into his lap…"not okay for me to take the treasure jar home."

Sara's mouth dropped open at his announcement. Under her breath she exclaimed, "No way!"

Astonished, Ray and Laura looked at each other. They both had the same thought. *Could Morgan have been damaged from his accident—maybe some undetected brain injury? And dreaming of this Native American boy over and over, what's that about?*

"Go on, Son," Ray said in a gentle tone. "Tell us what's going on with you."

"You'll probably think I'm crazy," Morgan said. Taking a deep breath and expelling it quickly, he continued, "But here goes anyway."

He ran his fingertips around the uneven rim of the pottery jar and cleared his throat. "You know about my dream friend. Well, we have so much fun hanging out together." He glanced up, sneaking a peek at his mom. "We go on adventures, and he tells me stuff about how his people lived. I like his stories."

"Yes, well, dreams sure can be exciting," Ray said, massaging an earlobe.

"Gotta tell all of it," Morgan thought. "Even about the vision quest and how I got my animal spirit name." Excitement threatened to burst from his chest at the memory.

But Morgan's smooth brow creased as he gently clamped his lower lip between his teeth thinking about Young Eagle's photograph in the library book.

"Dang," he thought, "will Mom and Dad laugh when I tell them that a long time ago, Young Eagle was a real person?"

"I'll wait till later," he decided silently, "to tell them."

After a moment Morgan said, "Well, at the lake a couple of important things happened. Can't remember if it was when I fell asleep on the dock," his voice turned whispery, "or later… maybe in the water."

"Anyway, Young Eagle explained the custom of his people for choosing a name, you know, for babies. They pick an ancestor's name. He also told me that when a boy reaches a certain age, he must go on a vision quest. You know, to learn how to become a proud brave and a good hunter. On this journey, he learns things to help him through life."

Morgan's expression became animated as he unraveled the story. His foot jiggled in double time. "I wanted a guardian animal spirit too, you know? So guess what? Young Eagle, helped me into a vision quest, and it happened! Can't tell you everything. Young Eagle said that would be my choice. But I can tell you about an experience I'll never forget."

"It's okay to keep some things to yourself," Ray interrupted. "Sorry. Go on, tell us what happened. This is getting interesting."

A troubled expression wavered in Morgan's eyes. "This is the part I've been afraid to tell you. Trust me, it's been torture."

Morgan continued slowly. "The whole day at the lake…so… I don't know…confusing and jumbled up." He shook his head slowly, "I think Young Eagle came when I was asleep in the lake, and took me on this incredible journey."

Morgan reached out and slid the jar closer. "And that's when I learned something about this treasure jar."

"Finally," Laura thought, "he's going to open up." But she was agitated at Morgan's version of his near-drowning. She reached over and grasped his forearm.

Morgan stared at his mom's hand.

Her fingers felt cold against his skin.

Then a sudden realization speared his thoughts. "Crystal Lake—an icy hand pulled me from danger. That had to be Young Eagle." *He rescued me! Not a lake-monster!*

"Earth to Morgan," Laura said snapping her fingers. "Where did you go?"

Smiling, Morgan, slowly shook his head, "Sorry. Just thinking about something."

Ray chuckled and said, "Glad you're back."

"Morgan, you were *unconscious* for a few minutes," Laura said.

"Mom's right," Ray said. "But in all fairness to you, I suppose being unconscious is like sleeping."

A smile tugged at the corner of Morgan's mouth. "Okay, how's this? When I was *unconsciously* sleeping in the water."

But from the expressions on his parents' faces, he knew the joke didn't fly.

"I know you all were worried for me," he said. "But I'm okay now. Really."

His parents gave him a reassuring smile.

"Well," Morgan continued, "Young Eagle appeared and wanted to have an adventure. We walked through the woods. He played a wooden flute and I shook something that rattled."

He gave Sara an impish smile. "Could have been the tail of a rattlesnake."

"*Morgan!*" cried Sara. "You're making that up."

Shrugging a shoulder, Morgan continued. "Anyway, we watched a beaver swim around with twigs in its mouth, searching for a place to make a home." A wistful smile curved his mouth. "It was the best time."

Morgan drained his glass of water. "I told him about Sara and me finding this jar and some arrowheads. Young Eagle asked me to describe the treasure jar.

"Kinda scary what he said next." A frown rippled his brow. "He said his people used jars like this as burial urns, for cremation ashes. He called my jar a...," Morgan swallowed. "...a Spirit Jar."

Morgan stared at the wall across the room. He pressed the back of his wrist against the tip of his nose and sniffed.

"Young Eagle told me that the ground where I found it was sacred and should never be disturbed."

Unease whispered through him as he waited for some kind of response.

Ray shot Laura a concerned look. He leaned back in his chair and locked his arms around his chest.

"Son, we won't make false promises. But, be assured, we can work this out," Ray said in a firm, yet sympathetic tone.

"Sweetie, your adventures with this Native American boy are dreams," Laura said.

"Believe me, I know how real they can seem. When I was oh, maybe ten, I had vivid dreams of performing in a circus! A trapeze artist, no less." She smiled, remembering. "A marquee over a huge tent advertised," she swept a hand in an arc, 'Princess of the Air' " Pressing her fingertips to her chest, she added, "Me of course.

"Now, try to imagine this. I swung high above crowds, clutching the hanging bar. Then I flipped over and caught the bar under my knees." For a moment Laura's eyes glazed as a mind-picture shimmered and died. She chuckled and said, "That was a fun dream."

Ray said, "I believe—and this is only an assumption on my

part—that while we sleep, maybe subconscious wishes come alive, sometimes in the most colorful way." A lopsided grin tugged at the corner of his mouth. "I really believe, a dream journal could be useful to you."

"I'm safe!" Morgan thought. "I can spill my guts." He chuckled under his breath. "Well some of 'em."

Morgan looked at his parents and said, "Get this. On this journey with Young Eagle, we were flying over a forest."

"Wow," said Sara, leaning forward, gripping the edges of her chair seat.

"Yeah," said Morgan. A remote expression leaked into his eyes as dream-memories sifted through his mind. He lowered his head and tucked his prayer-positioned hands between his quaking knees.

Laura sensed that Morgan had more to tell them. She rose from her chair. Standing behind him, she kneaded the stiffness trapped in his neck.

Ray reached out and gently lifted Morgan's chin. Peering into his son's trouble eyes, he asked, "There's more, isn't there?"

Morgan glanced away, whispering, "Yeah." His expression held confusion when he continued, "I couldn't actually see anything. Something…fog stuff covered my eyes. I tried not to be afraid because I was with Young Eagle, and he's really brave, you know. Then, even though I couldn't see where we were, I knew he had taken me to the place where Sara and I found the treasure. You know, under the juniper tree." He shook his head slowly, "I just knew it."

Morgan glanced around the table. "Look at them," he thought. "They think I've lost it."

Ray smiled. "I think I know what's going on here. You

want to get this," he nodded toward the jar, "back to sacred ground."

"Of course," Laura thought, "it's been so obvious." Her face beamed as she asked Morgan, "Is that what you would like, sweetheart?"

Overwhelmed with relief, Morgan released a huge sigh. "Yes! Yes, that's exactly it!"

Excitement set his leg jiggling in double time.

He spoke in a rush now, words tumbling into space.

"Dad, would you and Mom help me, please?" I know it's a long drive back to the campground and a lot to ask. But it's…it's, you know, important to me." His brow rippled as he added, "My promise…"

Laura slid her chair next to Morgan and circled her arms around his shoulders. "A perfect solution for the Spirit Jar," she said, "return it to where it belongs. We will all go back to the campground." She pulled away and pressed her hands against Morgan's flushed cheeks. "Of course you can keep your promise," she said, tenderly.

"You're a good kid, Morgan," said Ray. He coughed into a rolled fist. "We're proud of you. Don't worry, we'll work something out." He hesitated. "Let's see, this is Monday." He looked at Laura. "What do you think, honey? I mean timing— school and all."

She shrugged, turning both palms up. "How about Wednesday?"

A broad smile split Morgan's face. "All right!" he yelped and sprang from the chair. "You mean it? So Soon?"

"You bet," said Ray. He winked at Sara. "How about you, princess, want to go on a special trip?"

"*Yippee!* cried Sara, clapping her hands. Her face animated pleasure at this unexpected event. "Daddy, can we stay at least overnight? Could we, pleeeease?"

Ray chuckled. "Sure, I think we can manage a couple of nights. But we'd better get an early start." He glanced at Morgan. "Would four o'clock in the morning work for you?" He leaned back in his chair. "That would put us at the campground before nightfall."

Morgan blew a long breath. "That'll work." He reached for a slice of garlic bread. "Jeez, I was so worried. Didn't know how to tell you guys about my problem, you know?" Not waiting to breathe, he said, "I'm hungry. Can we eat now?"

"Yes," said Laura, "just give me a minute. The lasagna's ready to serve." As she removed a baking dish from the oven, she said, "I believe Friday is a teachers' day. There's no school. You will only miss two days. I'll call for assignments."

Morgan breathed in the spicy aroma of lasagna and daydreamed a minute, recalling the day he innocently dug the Spirit Jar from sacred ground.

Steam rose from the generous serving Laura placed before him. His taste buds kicked in and a genuine smile traveled to his eyes. "Looks good, Mom."

"Smells good too," Ray said, plucking a slice of warm garlic bread from a basket. "I've been thinking," he said, glancing at Morgan. "How would you feel about expressing an apology? Say, like a personal note to your dream friend, explaining our regret at disturbing sacred ground." He watched for Morgan's reaction to his suggestion. After a moment, he added, "Maybe burying it with the Spirit Jar?"

Morgan's tone rang with joy. "Yeah, Dad. I like it." But then a slight frown crinkled his brow as he chewed. "Don't know quite what to say, though."

"Good. You'll think of something," said Ray. He reached over and squeezed Morgan's shoulder. "Keep it simple but from your heart." He smiled at Laura. "The lasagna's terrific, honey."

"Thank you," said Laura. At that moment she recalled the conversation where Morgan had confided of tingling sensations when he held the Spirit Jar. "I'll share that with Ray this evening," she mused silently.

After Morgan finished his meal, he leaned back in his chair and closed his eyes. A glimpse of Young Eagle's face appeared—he was smiling.

"Earth to Morgan," Ray said into his son's ear. "You in there?"

Morgan blinked and stretched his arms overhead, "Yeah, just thinking."

Grinning, Ray asked, "Well, when you're finished, would you help me get some of the camping gear together tonight?"

"Sure, Dad. No problem."

"Great," said Ray. "We won't need much for a couple of nights. We can take the smaller tent, sleeping bags, and the cooking gear that we use for our day-hiking."

"Mommy, I can help you with the food we're taking," Sara offered, carrying her dinner plate to the sink.

"Great. Get a piece of paper and we can plan menus together."

Sara tore sheets of lined paper from a notebook. She selected pencils from a pink ceramic cup near the telephone.

"Pull your chair next to me," said Laura.

The kitchen door swung open. Morgan, soft-shoed across the linoleum.

Sara covered her face with her sheet of paper. "You are such a showoff, Morgan."

"Did you guys get our gear together?" asked Laura.

"Yo, Mom. Sure did," Morgan replied. He swooped toward Sara and tickled her ribs. She giggled and twisted away.

"Good," Laura answered and continued with her shopping list.

Sara waved notepaper in Laura's face. "See, Mommy, I put marshmallows and grahams on my list. Oh, almost forgot hot chocolate mix."

"Perfect," said Laura. "Now off to bed with you both."

After Morgan and Sara left the room, Ray asked, "What do you think of our son's vivid nighttime adventures?" Before she answered he added, "You looked perplexed while he told us about them."

"Hmmmm," said Laura as she leaned back in her chair. She drummed the paper with a pencil and cleared her throat.

"Well, at first I feared that he may have gotten a head injury from the horrible ordeal at the lake. And that maybe the doctor didn't discover something serious." She shook her head slightly. "Okay, this may sound kind of, to borrow one of Morgan's favorite adjectives, weird. But could this dream boy, Young Eagle, be connected with the treasure jar—I mean Spirit Jar? He says they began at the campground. So, just maybe, in his sleeping mind, a spirit…I don't know…crashed into his subconscious? Does that sound crazy or what?"

"Anything's possible," said Ray. Locking his arms across his chest, he added, "You could have something there."

As they entered their bedroom, Ray said, "I like the idea of putting the Spirit Jar back in the earth, where it belongs."

Laura folded the bedspread back and fluffed her pillow. Through a yawn, she said, "I agree. It's perfect."

Ray eased under the covers, saying, "Night, my love."

As Laura slid into sleep, three whispery words caressed her ear: *Help! I'm alone.*

By morning, she would not remember the mystifying message.

But soon, the wilderness will unveil another treasure—just in time.

Chapter Twenty-three

Shades of tangerine and rose water-colored the morning sky as a slice of sun peeked over the eastern hills.

Awake before dawn, Morgan lay listening to a frog-duo croaking under his window. Too excited to sleep, he scrambled out of his warm covers, and wandered into the kitchen.

"Good morning, young man," said Ray. Newspaper rustled as he folded a section. Peering over his reading classes, he said, "Don't want to nag about your hair, but maybe you could give some thought to a haircut when we get back?" A hint of a smile traveled to his eyes.

Morgan raked his fingers through his dark, shaggy hair. He eased into a chair and scrubbed his eyelids.

"Yeah, Dad, I know. I just thought it'd be cool to have a ponytail first day of school." He scooped a bundle of hair toward his nape. Several strands flopped over his forehead. "But it's not long enough and kinda hot on my neck." He folded his arms on the table, giving his dad a lopsided grin. Drumming his fingertips on the table, he asked, "Mom, what's for breakfast?"

"Are you excited about the trip?" she asked. Not waiting for an answer, she said, "Eggs or cereal, which would you like?"

Morgan raised his arms overhead and punched the air with his fists. "I can't wait. And you guys have been great—about everything." Scrubbing his palms together, he asked, "Scrambled eggs and toast, please?"

"You got it," said Laura.

"You must have been stewing over the Spirit Jar dilemma a lot," Laura said as she cracked eggs into a bowl.

"Yeah," Morgan replied quietly. Before he'd left his bedroom that morning, he had taken the Young Eagle photograph off the door and tucked it in the back of the notebook he planned on using as his journal. "Maybe someday I'll figure out a rational explanation for this...this mystery," he thought.

Ray reached over and squeezed the back of Morgan's neck. "Everything's settled now, kid. You can stop worrying."

Sara, clad in lavender pajamas stenciled with mermaids, wandered into the kitchen. In a sleepy voice, she said, "Hi, everybody."

"Come here, sweet girl. Give me a hug," Laura said.

"I've been thinking," said Ray, glancing over at Morgan, "about the apology note. Your grandpa gave me some advice when I was young and had confusing situations. He said, 'Son, just think from your heart.'" He smiled at the memory. "It's worked for me."

Morgan slid his empty plate aside and braced a hand under his chin. "I don't know what to say, Dad," He shrugged a shoulder. "Guess I have a lot to think about."

"You'll do fine," Ray said with a reassuring smile.

"If you say so."

Ray looked at his watch. "I gotta go."

"Bye, Daddy," Sara said as she poured milk over a bowl of cereal.

Laura gave Ray a quick kiss. "See you later." Looking at Morgan, she said, "That was good advice your grandpa had to offer. Like Dad told you, Morgan, you'll work it out." Glancing at the kitchen clock, she said, "Scoot, it's about time for you guys to get ready for school."

Laura stood in the kitchen doorway, watching Morgan wrap his arms around his sister's waist, then lift her and strut like a penguin. After a few feet, Sara went limp as a rag doll and slid from his grip. She scuttled on her hands and knees toward her bedroom.

"Thanks for the ride, Bro."

Morgan grabbed one of Sara's fuzzy pink slippers and lobbed it overhand, bopping her on the head.

"Thanks a lot," Sara scoffed. "I thought you were going to be nice for a change."

"Bull's-eye!" cried Morgan. He made a face, entered his room, and closed the door.

"Take it easy, Sara," Laura said, tapping lightly on the closed door. "I set out some clothes for you to wear today. Hurry up."

Sometime later, a horn tooted, signaling the arrival of the school bus.

"Later, Mom," Morgan called over his shoulder as he rushed out the door.

"Sara, do you want a ride to school?" Laura asked.

"I'm meeting Jane. We'll walk, thanks anyway, Mommy."

"You're welcome," said Laura.

❧   ❧   ❧

After dinner that evening, Morgan sat at the dining room table, hovered over a yellow tablet, its green lines bare. A slight frown creased his brow, and his mouth twisted in concentration as he waited for inspiration.

He slumped in his chair.

"This is not going to be easy," he said under his breath.

"What 'cha doing?" Sara asked, climbing onto a chair beside him.

Startled by her interruption, he said, "Dang, Sara, do you have to sneak up on me all the time? Get lost!"

Sara's shoulder pressed against his arm as she reached and tried to grab the tablet. "You don't have to be such a weenie!"

Morgan whipped the tablet out of her reach, flagging it over his head. "Just get out of here. I'm busy."

"Okay, be a weirdo. See if I care," said Sara. She slid from the chair and stomped out of the room.

"Whatever," Morgan muttered, circling an arm around the pad of yellow paper. After a few minutes, he began to write. When he finished, he tore the page off, folded it carefully, and stuffed the note into a back pocket of his jeans.

Morgan eased from his chair and joined his parents in the kitchen.

"Say, young man, did you finish your project?" said Ray as he raised his coffee mug and sipped, his eyebrows lifting in question.

Morgan shifted from one foot to the other, giving his parents a lazy smile. "Would it be okay if I keep what I wrote a secret?"

"Secret?" Sara said, rolling her eyes. "Why can't we hear what you wrote?"

"Because it's between Young Eagle and me. That's why."

Laura said, "Your brother's right this time, honey. It's private."

"You know, Morgan," said Ray, "you gave us a gift by sharing your dreams of Young Eagle." He chuckled as he added, "Truth is, your dream friend woke us up!" He leaned back smiling at his humor. "Anyway, some artifacts are best left behind."

Laura's eyes glazed with tears. "I was thinking about my parents' graves. What if someone had damaged their grave markers?" A melancholy expression clung to her face like a mask. "You both were young and don't remember the auto accident that killed them both." A shudder whipped through her torso. "I spent the night before the burial service writing a letter to each of them, acknowledging loving moments we had spent together."

As his Mom verbalized her anguish, Morgan leaned forward and folded his arms on the table. Resting his chin on his stacked forearms, he closed his eyes.

A scene came into focus.

He was about five years old, standing in the driveway, watching Grandpa Ben wash a car. They were laughing because his grandpa had lost the grip on the hose, and water whipped everywhere, soaking them both. If he thought hard enough, he could see his Grandma Marie's smiling eyes. And smell the scent of the fresh-baked bread that she made almost every day.

Sitting at the kitchen table, listening quietly to her mother's story, Sara patiently hooked bright multicolored paper clips together. She arranged her handiwork in a circle on the table. Grinning with satisfaction, she tilted her head from side to side and said, "It's big enough." She slid from her chair and offered the variegated circle to her mother.

Laura pressed one hand over the other against her chest. She gave her daughter a tender smile. "Oh, sweetie, it's beautiful." She leaned forward and asked, "May I wear it?"

Eyes wide with pride, Sara nodded and slipped the loop over her mother's bent head. "Think I'll make another one."

Morgan laughed. "Yeah, Sara, you could probably sell 'em at the swap meet."

"I'm sure," Sara retorted. "Besides, I know you're just teasing me. I *meant* that I'm going to make one for my bear."

"Whatever," said Morgan, shrugging a shoulder.

"Let's appreciate your sister's creative efforts," said Laura.

Morgan fingered the colorful necklace. "Looks kinda nice on Mom."

Ray rose to his feet. He gave Morgan a playful cuff on the shoulder and winked his approval.

"Let's not get sidetracked, guys," said Ray. He reached for the Spirit Jar. "We have to go on a special journey tomorrow."

The aged clay felt cold against Ray's palms.

He handed the jar to Morgan. "Here you go. You're in charge."

"Thanks, Dad."

Morgan filled a glass with water and drank thirstily. "Guess I'll go to bed now."

"Night, Son. See you in the morning—like daybreak?"

"That'll work," said Morgan.

"Better pack that black down-filled jacket, Morgan," said Laura. "It'll be colder this trip. Sleep well, sweetie."

He turned at the doorway. "I will. And thanks, you know for…"

Laura smiled. "You're welcome. Your dad and I are happy

we were able to help."

"Sara," Laura said, "I'll tuck you in when you're ready."

"Okay, Mommy," said Sara as she skipped down the hall.

After bedtime rituals were complete and the house quiet, Ray sat on the edge of the bed and set the radio alarm clock. He switched off the bedside lamp saying, "Good night."

"Sleep well," Laura murmured. "See you in the morning—early."

"You bet," said Ray.

Chapter Twenty-four

Anxious to start the trip, Morgan had spent most of the night twisting and turning, under the comforter.

"I didn't even have a dream with Young Eagle," he said in a disappointed tone.

"Dang. Isn't it time to get up yet?"

Morgan flipped onto his side and squinted at the digital clock on the bedside table. "Four o'clock. I'm getting up," he said, flipping the comforter aside.

Down the hall, Morgan's parents were startled awake by a loud buzzing from the clock-radio.

Laura rolled onto her side, reached over, and silenced the intruding noise.

She placed a hand on Ray's shoulder and whispered, "Are you awake?"

"Yeah, think so," said Ray. Brushing his hands over his tousled hair, he blinked at the clock. "Time to rise and shine," he crooned.

"Yup," said Laura.

She sat up, slid her feet to the floor, and shrugged into a

light blue fleece robe.

Before stepping into the hall, she said, "Breakfast on the road?"

Through a yawn, Ray said, "Sounds like a plan."

He lay without moving, eyes closed, until the aroma of brewing coffee spurred him into action.

Chilly air raised goose bumps on his flesh as he pulled on blue jeans. He grabbed a sweatshirt and padded barefoot down the hall, humming softly.

Morgan, already dressed, greeted him in the kitchen.

Sara, after some persuasion and Laura's help, was ready to leave within the hour.

ᐠᐠ   ᐠᐠ   ᐠᐠ

As Ray backed the van out of the driveway, a reddish glow tickled the rolling hills that surrounded the town.

A cardboard box lay on the backseat between Morgan and Sara. The container held the Spirit Jar, nestled in crumpled newspaper. Morgan's arm rested protectively on the top. An absent expression claimed his eyes as he stared out the side window.

Sara, slumped beneath her seat belt, dozed through the early morning drive.

They had been traveling awhile when Ray said, "We're going to need gas soon." Massaging the muscle of his thigh, he added, "There's a mileage sign ahead. See how many miles to the next town."

Laura removed her sunglasses to get a clear view. "Slow down a bit—Rosehill, ten miles." She reached over and gently kneaded the back of his neck. "Ready for a break?"

"Sure am. I'm hungry too. How about you?"

"Yes, I'm famished. We can fill up and find a place for breakfast."

A two-lane asphalt road led to the rural town of Rosehill. Groups of tawny cows grazed on pastureland. Distant farmhouses dotted the landscape. An occasional deep red barn brightened the wheat-colored hills.

The family preferred, when traveling, to visit towns away from the interstate highway. They enjoyed eating in cafes where the locals hung out. The food, most of the time, was better, and the atmosphere always interesting.

Rosehill's main street consisted of four blocks. Buildings that were built a hundred years ago still stood. Mom - and - pop shops were open for business.

The only gas station in town occupied half the first block. Ray parked beside one of the two gas pumps.

In the next block, across the street, Laura pointed toward a pink neon sign flashing the words Caboose Café. "Now that's the place for breakfast. I like it," she said. "Let's stop."

"That'll work," said Ray as he drove away from the gas station.

He parked in a gravel parking area, in front of the restaurant.

Morgan peered through the side window. "Cool."

"It's a train," said Sara.

"This is a caboose car that's been converted into a café," said Ray. "I see they have maintained the dull wine-red color and black trim. And they've added windows along the side. Well, let's go in and see what's happening around this town."

The aroma of fresh-brewed coffee, fried sausage, and sweet pastries curled around them, tantalizing their hunger.

Three men, clad in denim overalls and perched on stools at

a small counter, glanced around to see who was coming in the door. Behind the counter, a woman poured coffee and laughed at something one of them had said.

"Morning, folks. Come on in. Booths are back there and menus are on the table," said the woman.

There were four booths, all empty. Sara chose one and slid across the padded, red vinyl seat.

"This is charming," Laura said. She tilted her head toward the pint milk bottles, stuffed with flowers, which adorned each table.

The woman who greeted them squeezed her plump figure through an opening by the cash register. She approached with a pot of coffee and a smile. Over her shoulder she cautioned in a cheerful tone, "You boys behave, now." She wore a green sweatshirt over black pants. Embroidered white daisy flowers rambled across her ample bosom. Two lime-colored mugs clinked as she set them on the table.

"Bet you kids would like hot chocolate," the hostess said, winking at Sara. "Coffee okay for you, mom and dad?"

Laura extended a grateful smile and said, "You bet."

Ray lifted one of the mugs. Through a laugh, he breathed, "Pour away, you angel. We've been on the road since dawn."

Her round face split with a wide grin. "My name's Hazel. Where you folks from? I know everybody around these parts. You aren't local."

Laura handed a menu to Ray. "We're from Woodlake, a town south of here." She looked around the room, admiring the antique railroad memorabilia on the walls and shelves. "You have a nice place here. Was this a railroad town at one time?"

Morgan looked out the small window. "Mom, check it out,

no tracks."

An amused expression spread into Hazel's brown eyes. "Observant young man. Actually, the railroad station was located in the next town, about twenty miles east of here. It's been closed for years. After my father retired from the railroad company, they surplussed a number of these caboose cars. He bought one and had it moved to this location, but he didn't know what to do with it. I figured it's just the right size for a coffee shop." She looked at Morgan as she settled her hands on her ample hips. "Kinda cool, huh?"

One of the locals from the group at the counter carried a tray with two mugs of steaming liquid to the table. Fragrant hot chocolate and a saucer of marshmallows piqued Sara's attention.

"Here ya go, kids," said the local man.

Sara's mouth gaped as she stared at the mound of puffy confections. She glanced up. "How did you know I love marshmallows?"

The man winked at Laura and rubbed his whiskered chin as he looped a thumb around a strap of his denim overalls. "Just a lucky guess. It's hot, though, so sip slow."

As he turned to join the group at the counter, Hazel said, "Thanks Charlie."

Across the room, huddled in a corner, sat a shiny chrome box the size of a refrigerator.

"Hey," Morgan said. "A jukebox."

"Sure is," said Hazel. She arched an eyebrow, "It works too. Put a quarter in and you get three selections of great forties and fifties music." She raised a plump arm, waving it around the room. "All this is stuff my dad collected throughout his career as a railroad conductor." She sighed. "I miss him."

Ray nodded in sympathy. "It's nice to have all these memories of him though."

"And we're enjoying this café and your hospitality," Laura added.

Hazel reached into her apron pocket for an order pad. Fingering her large, gray-streaked bun, she found a stubby pencil.

"Thanks for the compliment," she said. Recollections of her father carried a smile into her eyes. "I do enjoy this place. I feel his presence everyday. Now, what are you all having this morning?"

Morgan wandered around the room, and stopped at a counter of assorted railroad mementoes.

His heart surged at what he saw. Hidden behind a pile of souvenir picture postcards, lay a miniature bow and quiver of arrows. A perfect duplicate of the one that Young Eagle carried.

"That's it," Morgan thought. "Instead of a dream last night, Young Eagle left a treasure for me today!"

Hazel walked over to Morgan. "Your parents ordered breakfast for you," she said.

Before turning away, something caught her attention.

"Well, what do you know," said Hazel. "I thought…" She picked up the tiny bow and quiver of arrows. "I haven't seen these…," she said, slowly shaking her head, "for a *long* time. I thought they were lost forever."

Morgan glanced up at Hazel, musing silently, "But I know why they're here now. Young Eagle performed magic—just for me!"

"Do you want to know a secret, young man?" Hazel whispered.

"Sure," Morgan replied softly.

"Well, some mornings when I open this place, I find one of the mementoes that my father collected—moved. I keep it to my self, though. I just put them back. I believe it's his way of saying, "I'm here, Darlin'. Don't be sad.""

After a moment she said, "My dad would sit for hours polishing his railroad car collection and telling me stories of his life as a railroad conductor.

"Would you like to have these?" asked Hazel, holding the miniature bow and quiver of arrows in the palm of her hand.

"*Really!?*" asked Morgan.

"Yes," Hazel replied, "I have a hunch they belong with you."

"Thanks. Thanks a lot," Morgan breathed, as he wrapped his unexpected gift in a paper napkin.

He smiled up at Hazel, before he turned to join his family.

Sliding into the booth, Morgan said, "I've got something to show you."

Chapter Twenty-five

By the time they arrived at the campground, the sun had dipped behind the mountains. A few scattered campfires warmed the dusky scene

Laura took a hesitant step away from the van. Silently, she counted to ten wondering if the White Feather tribe's spirits or ghosts had left—until next year.

"Hmm, seems normal," she thought. Out loud she said, "Brrrr. It is colder this trip. But it's great to be back."

"Sure is," Ray said. Glancing in Morgan's direction, he said, "I'll handle the tent. You can get our sleeping bags so we can get bedded down and out of the cold."

Sara, perched on her rolled sleeping bag inside the van, asked, "Mommy, am I sleeping in here with you?"

Laura grunted as she moved a box of supplies to the front seat. "Yes, sweetie. We girls will be comfy in here. The guys can rough it in the tent."

As nightfall seeped into the forest, the temperature plunged.

Early next morning, Laura awoke to the scent of a campfire wafting through a slightly open window.

"Ahh," she said, stretching her legs and wiggling her toes. "Sara, "I think it's time to get up."

Enveloped in her sleeping bag, Sara answered in a muffled tone, "I'm awake, Mommy." She pushed thick fabric from her face. "Cuddle me. I'm cold."

"Silly girl," said Laura. "It's warm as toast in these bags." She nuzzled her face into the soft fabric. "C' mon, let's get by that cheery fire your daddy has going."

Sara slowly emerged from her warm cocoon.

A tap on the window drew her attention. Ray's face pressed against the glass, flattened his nose. Vapor spread out the sides of his mouth as he breathed, fogging the cold glass.

"Look at Daddy," Sara said, pressing her palm against the window. "He's so goofy."

Laura beamed a smile at Ray and said, "Good morning. Got coffee?"

"You bet," said Ray. He pushed away from the window. "It's a great day for a hike."

Laura emerged from the van, tipped her eyes toward a cloudless, cobalt sky, and breathed in crisp mountain air. "You are right," she said, "it is a glorious fall day."

Morgan stood at the picnic table and opened the cardboard box containing the Spirit Jar. "Can we leave right after breakfast?"

"Definitely okay by me," Laura said. "And since we're here, I'd like to stop by and say hello to Mr. Harold. I never thought we'd return this year." she paused a moment. "You know, Morgan, you could write about these trips in your journal."

"Already started," Morgan said. He pulled a spiral notebook

from the box. "I copied my apology note on the first page."

Morgan turned toward Sara. With a reproachful frown, he said, "This book is out of bounds—get it? No snooping."

She gave him a withering look. "I have better things to do than to read your stupid journal." Tossing a wrapped granola bar, in his direction, she added, "You better stop looking for my diary too."

"All right, all right. It's a deal," said Morgan.

"Well, I'm happy you two worked that one out," Laura said.

"Way to go, Morgan," Ray said, removing his leather gloves. "Glad you chose my journal suggestion. I predict you will find it quite valuable when you get older."

❧   ❧   ❧

After breakfast, Ray whistled softly as he hitched the straps of his backpack over his shoulders. He tucked the camp shovel under his arm. "Do you still have the compass, Morgan?"

"Yo, Dad," Morgan answered. He tugged a string from the neck of his sweatshirt. "Right here."

"Great idea," said Ray. Turning toward Laura, he asked, "Do you have the flashlight? We might need it on our way back."

"Sure do," said Laura. Sliding a white painter's cap over her hair, she asked, "Sara do you need any help?"

Sara struck a model's pose, exclaiming, "Ta-daah! See? My red boots and this rain hat match my backpack."

Laura laughed and said, "Cute. Where on earth did you find those boots and that funky hat?"

"In my closet," said Sara. She pulled the brim over her eyes.

Laura frowned. "Are those boots a snug enough fit, for the hike?"

"They're good, Mommy. I'm wearing my thick fuzzy socks."

"Well, okay," Laura said. After a moment she asked, "Do you kids have jackets?"

Morgan and Sara answered in unison, "Yes."

"Okay, guys, let's hit the road," Ray said, leading the way. "We have a full day ahead of us."

Bronze oak leaves, shed overnight, crunched as they walked down a narrow hiking path. Branches, heavy with pinecones, sagged over their heads.

Musky aroma from rotting logs, carpeted in dark green moss, smudged the air. Sun rays, sneaking through the overhead canopy, pleased the eye. Black, hairy bumblebees droned, landing heavily on drooping, end-of-the-summer wildflowers that were ready to surrender to chilly fall. Any one of these memories would bring an instant recall of this day.

But, the strongest reminder would be, the mysterious event about to unfold.

Chapter Twenty-six

When the steep, winding trail seemed unfamiliar to Ray, he stopped and planted a booted foot high on the rocky path. To steady himself, he leaned a shoulder against a tree trunk. Winded from climbing, he panted short breaths as he glanced around, his face etched in a puzzled expression.

"Now, wait a minute," Ray said as he reached into a back pocket for the hiking guide. After perusing the hand-drawn map from the previous trip, he shook his head. "No wonder nothing seems familiar. We camped in a different site this trip. There are two trails to the river. Sorry for the oversight guys."

He reached up, removed his cap, and combed his fingers through his hair. In a low voice, he asked Laura, "You okay to go on?"

Laura swiped a sleeved arm across her sweaty forehead. "Whew, this trail is steep." A large, jagged rock supported her from skidding backward down the dirt trail. "I'm fine," she said. Her eyes narrowed as she peered at the summit a few yards ahead. "We'll get our workout today."

"Those kids," said Ray, "they're already at the top." He issued a throaty chuckle. "Just like a couple of mountain goats."

Morgan stood on the crested incline. He cupped his hands around his mouth and called out, "Mom, Dad. You gotta see this." He whipped off his red baseball cap. "We've got trouble."

Her arms crossed over her chest, Sara gripped her hunched shoulders, her expression grim.

"We better get up there," Laura said. "Morgan sounded frightened."

"WE'RE ON OUR WAY," Ray shouted. He turned and grasped Laura's outstretched hand, steadying her.

Ray dug his boot heels into loose dirt, and climbed up the steep incline.

Laura grabbed exposed roots and ground shrubs, staying close to Ray.

At the top of the ridge, Ray reached down and grasped Laura's hand. He pulled her to him.

"What's up?" Ray asked.

Morgan's hand trembled slightly as he pointed down the trail. The path wandered into a wide curve, then traveled parallel to the ridge where they were standing.

"I hope its alive," he whispered.

Chapter Twenty-seven

Breathless, Laura asked, "What—"

"Over there," Morgan interrupted in a low tone. He grasped her arm. "See near that curve."

Ray crouched, his hands fisted against his thighs. Through a whisper, he said, "I see it."

"Oh no," Laura said through her steepled fingertips pressed against her chin. "What in the world is it doing up here? Alone."

Sara fixed Ray with worried brown eyes. In a plaintive tone she asked, "What can we do, Daddy?"

"Unbelievable," Ray said as he pushed to his feet, shaking his head in wonder. He frowned and shrugged out of his backpack. "I'd better see what's what. Has it moved at all?"

Morgan screwed his baseball cap onto his head, flipping the brim backward. "No," he answered. He lowered his head, studying his shoes. "Do you think…" Morgan started to ask, drawing a deep breath. "…You know?"

Ray reached over and ran a hand up and down Morgan's back. "Let's just see. Okay?"

He swallowed. "Okay, Dad."

Laura maneuvered between Morgan and Sara, draping arms across their shoulders. Giving them each a quick hug, she said, "Let Dad handle this. Maybe it's..." Her throat tightened over the unfinished sentence.

"You guys wait here," Ray said, smiling reassurance. "If there are wounds, he may not be in a friendly mood."

❧   ❧   ❧

A large dog lay on its side beside the path. Tan and black fur blended into the dirt and foliage that surrounded its motionless body.

Eager to go with his dad, Morgan tried to pull away from Laura's firm grip.

Ray bent over, grabbed a dried root, and stepped onto the steep trail. Out of the corner of his eye, he saw Morgan start toward him.

"No, Son. You need to stay here."

"I know, I know," Morgan answered in a reluctant tone. "But call me if you need me."

Ray nodded. "You got it."

When he was within a few feet of the prone body, the dog raised its head slightly and blinked, startling Ray momentarily.

He stepped forward and knelt beside the animal. In a low tone, he said, "Well now, what are you doing here all alone?"

Ray reached out slowly and stroked a forepaw. The tip of a pink, velvety tongue licked his fingertips.

Crouched on the grassy brow of the hill, elbows on his thighs, Morgan smiled when he saw what was happening. Cutting a look up at his mother, he pleaded, "Could I go down there now? I'll be careful."

After some hesitation, Laura answered, "Okay. But do what Dad tells you. Wait a minute." From her backpack, she fished a white plastic box with the Red Cross symbol stenciled on the lid. "Take this."

Grinning, Morgan said, "I'll be cool, Mom."

Taking a shortcut, Morgan slid on his backside down the embankment. Scrambling to his feet, he quickly made his way down the incline and crouched beside his dad.

"Mom sent this first aid stuff," he said.

"Good," said Ray. "We'll probably need it."

Whimpering and too weak to sit up, the dog's gold-flecked brown eyes tracked this new voice.

Morgan said quietly, "Hello there. Did you get lost?"

The dog didn't flinch as Ray probed its hip area.

"I don't think anything's broken, or he would have yelped," Ray said as he examined the animal's feet. "Aha. Here's one problem." Dirt and dried blood matted its pads. "Easy boy," Ray said as he lifted one of the dog's hind legs to check for injury to the stomach area. He chuckled. *"Hello!* you're not a fella—you're a lady!"

"Hope she'll be okay," said Morgan. "I'm worried for her."

"Morgan, open that kit and hand me some of those gauze squares. There's a tube of medicated salve in there too." He glanced at the open lid, "Oh good, give me that sponge."

"I'll wet it," Morgan offered. He pulled a water bottle from his backpack. A compressed object the size of a sliver of soap expanded like magic into an oval sponge, as water soaked the fiber.

Ray dribbled water and gently massaged away the dirt and dried blood caked on the animal's paw pads.

The dog licked the moisture dripping from Ray's hands.

"Cup your hand and pour in a bit of water," Ray told Morgan.

"Good idea, Dad. Here you go, girl."

Ray applied a generous coating of salve onto each pad. "Hope we can get her on her feet," he said. "These wounds aren't too deep. The salve should numb the abrasions." Through a sigh he added, "But, she's very weak."

Morgan sprang to his feet. "I could make a travois to carry her. You know, like the Native Americans."

Looking around, Morgan said, "There's loads of stuff we can use."

Jamming his hands into his jean pockets, he added, "Young Eagle and I made one. It'd be easy."

Before Ray could respond, Laura called out, "How's the dog? Is it hurt badly?"

Loud enough for her to hear, Ray said, "Doesn't seem too bad. By the way, it's a female."

"Hang in there, girl," Morgan said. "Maybe if we let her rest…"

Wiping salve from his fingers, Ray said, "We did all we could for now. Guess we'll just wait and see." He waved a signal for Laura and Sara to join them.

Sara crouched beside her brother and said, "Hi, doggie. Do you hurt much?"

She reached out timidly and picked a pine needle from the animal's long, tangled fur.

Laura squatted next to Sara and stroked the top of the dog's head. A half-smile touched her lips. "You sure are a ragged looking puppy." Massaging the dog's ruff, she commented, "No collar. She must have been wandering for days."

"I couldn't feel much fat under the mass of tangled fur," said Ray. "She may have trouble walking. If that's the case, Morgan has an excellent idea for transporting her."

"Wait," said Morgan as he rummaged through his backpack, careful not to disturb his precious cargo, the Spirit Jar. He plucked out a package of beef jerky. "Look—perfect."

Scenting food, the dog snuffled the sealed package.

"Just a minute, girl," said Morgan. He tore it open and pulled out a dark brown strip. "Here ya go."

The dog gulped down the treat and thumped the tip of her tail against the dirt path, begging for more.

After Morgan and Sara fed a few pieces to the hungry animal, Ray said, "Best to go easy on the food, kids. Give her a little more water, then let's see if we can fix it so she can walk."

Speaking to Morgan, Ray said, "If we have to resort to your travois idea, you may want to get started."

Morgan gave his father a broad smile and said, "I just happen to have my Swiss Army knife with me."

"All right!" said Ray. "You're well prepared for this emergency."

Using the saw-blade tucked in the knife, Morgan cut and stripped leaves from several slender branches.

He began to untie the shoelaces from his Reeboks.

Laura cried, *"Morgan! Your shoes will fall off."*

"It's okay, Mom. Don't worry. I don't really need the laces."

He reached into the neck of his sweatshirt and pulled out the compass that was attached to thick string. "See? I can use this string and these shoelaces to lash the cross-poles together with the base. You know, like a bed. We can use my sweatshirt as a pad."

"Well, all right," said Laura in a wary tone.

Morgan laid several branches on the ground, side by side, about four inches apart. He placed a few more across them, creating a checkerboard effect.

He stood beside his project a moment, a perplexed expression darkening his eyes.

"We only have one problem," Morgan said, frowning. "No horse to pull the travois."

"Yeah. No horse," Sara said between a string of giggles.

Morgan ignored his sister's mocking.

"Hey. I got it," said Morgan, giving Sara a wide mischievous grin. "We could just hitch *you* up to the travois!" Patting his rump, he said, "Giddyup horsy!"

Clamping her arms across her chest, Sara scowled, saying, "You are so not funny, Morgan."

"That's enough teasing," said Ray.

"The travois was a good idea, Morgan," Laura said. "But I think after your dad finishes doctoring her, she's going to be fine."

"Hope so," Morgan said.

Ray wrapped each paw in gauze, forming white slippers. "Attagirl," he coaxed as he secured each one with tape. "You're a brave puppy."

Fondling the tip of a furry ear, Sara said, "I wonder where she belongs? She needs brushing. There's tons of twigs and burrs in her fur." Picking at the debris, she said, "Oh, poor thing, you lost your family."

Laura watched Sara, groom the scruffy animal. Her eyes glazed with a flickering memory of herself as a child, playing with her pet dog. She shook her head as a nostalgic smile slowly emerged and the name "Annie" slipped out like a sigh.

Stroking the top of the dog's head Laura asked, "May we call you Annie as long as you're with us?"

The animal responded with a soft whine.

Laura mouthed "thank you," then stood and helped Sara to her feet.

"So, Annie it is," said Ray, "at least for now."

After a moment Laura said, "She could belong to someone in the campground or a family fishing along the riverbank…"

"What're we gonna do if we can't find anyone to claim her?" Morgan asked in a voice tinted with hope. He lowered his head, and studied a pinecone near his foot. "We could keep her." He looked askance at Laura. "I mean…she's friendly… and…and…I'd take care of her. She could even sleep on the back porch."

Sara sprang to her feet. "Oh, could we keep her?" she asked in a plaintive tone. "I just know she wouldn't be any trouble." Tilting her head back, she gripped Laura's hand. Her four-foot frame bobbed up and down on tiptoes, impatient for a favorable response. "We even have a fenced backyard. Please, please, could we?"

"Whoa there, kids," Ray said. "We need to talk about this. You know, she may only be temporary in our life." A frown rippled his brow as he glanced toward Laura for help.

Laura nodded agreement. "First, we have to make an effort to find the owner. Someone must be very sad because they lost this nice dog. Let's see if she can walk on those slippers Dad made."

Morgan stood by the unfinished travois, waiting.

"Lost Annie" struggled to a half-sitting position and nuzzled a gauze-covered paw. She sniffed and licked Morgan's outstretched hand.

Morgan, hated to admit his Mom was right.

He scratched the dog under the chin and said, "Okay, okay, I know. But if we can't find where she belongs, can we take her home with us?"

Laura poured water into Ray's cupped hands. He lowered the impromptu water bowl, and the dog lapped thirstily.

"We'll see what happens," said Ray. "Now, let's see if we can get her up on all fours."

With coaxing, the dog wobbled to her gauze-encased feet.

Morgan bent over and said, "You're okay, Annie. Come, I'll help you."

Sara pressed her hands to her lips, suppressing the urge to laugh as the dog awkwardly lifted each numbed paw like a puppet tap-dancing on a hot bed of coals.

"Wish I had a camcorder," Morgan said.

Ray chuckled, "Guess she's not feeling much pain."

"I wonder how old she is?" Laura mused aloud.

"A vet could tell," said Ray. He drank from a water bottle, capped it, and swiped a forearm across his mouth. Extending the bottle, he asked, "Want some?"

"Thanks," said Laura as she took the bottle. Her expression dubious, she said, "I hope those kids don't get too attached to her—at least not yet, anyway."

"I know," said Ray. He circled an arm around her shoulders and pulled her close. "It'll work out. They may not want to search for Annie's owners, but they know the drill." He rubbed his whisker-stubbled chin. "They know we have to make a sincere effort. At least I hope they understand."

Laura shrugged and squeezed his hand.

As they made their way down the trail, Morgan stopped often saying words of encouragement. Sara, guided the animal

from behind, hands pressed on each side of Annie's rump. Ray
and Laura, amused by the scene, hid smiles as they followed
a few feet behind.

"This hike may take longer than we planned," Laura said.

"How is our time?" Ray asked. "We didn't figure on finding
a dog in distress."

Laura narrowed her eyes and peered at her wristwatch. "It's
early. Plenty of daylight left."

Chapter Twenty-eight

The mountain trail spilled into a field, bare of trees, except for one enormous, sprawling pine standing sentinel near the middle. Branches spread like wings, heavy with green pinecones resembling baby pineapples.

Sunshine splashed around them as they walked toward the tree.

"Listen," said Ray. He cupped his hand around an ear. "Hear it?"

Crouching beside the dog, Morgan scratched Annie under her chin. "We're almost there," he said quietly.

Sara squeezed her eyelids tight, scrunching her lips into a bundle.

"The river!" she cried, pointing toward a curtain of dark green foliage. "It's over there."

"You're right," said Laura. "The sound is faint, but I hear water tumbling over rocks."

Ray knelt beside Morgan, and asked, "How's she doing with those slippers?"

"Good, Dad," said Morgan. He lowered his head and bit his

lower lip, stuffing unexpressed wishes in his throat. In half a day, part of his heart clung to this dog.

"You're a good girl," Morgan murmured. He pushed to his feet and cleared his throat. "Guess I'm ready."

"Well," said Ray, "we better get on with it. We're not far from the sacred place." He squeezed Morgan's shoulder. "The reason we're here."

Morgan sighed. "Yeah. I know, Dad."

Laura squatted, resting her elbows on her thighs. She plucked a blade of grass.

"You know, there's a sad family somewhere," Laura said, glancing at the dog, "missing this orphaned Annie."

"I know, Mom," said Morgan. Hope—for what may be impossible—flared in his chest as he rushed on, "But I just *know* Annie could live with us forever."

"Oh, the optimism of youth," Laura mused silently. "We'll just have to wait and see," she said, to Morgan.

"Okay, kids," Ray said. "We better get going now."

꩜   ꩜   ꩜

As they approached the lone pine tree, no one noticed a bald eagle circle and land on a dead, gray branch projecting from the top of the thick pine branches. Dark brown wings, fringed with white, slowly collapsed as the eagle's shiny, black talons gripped the dry wood. Several soft coo sounds flowed from its throat, as if to summon a lost friend. Its keen eyes watched the family as they hiked toward the river.

Morgan and Sara wandered ahead, Annie wobbling between them.

Pine trees shaded the bank of the river, where they decided to rest and have a snack. Morgan fed Annie beef jerky. Sara found a discarded plastic cup and filled it with water. Ray studied the trail map while he munched graham crackers. "Okay, I have our location pinpointed." Flagging the map, he said, "If we head in that direction, maybe we'll come across some fishermen and we can ask about…" Gazing down at Annie, he folded the map and tucked it into a back pocket. "We'll just follow the trail and see what happens."

Laura's shoulders sagged as she polished an apple. "Sometimes it's hard to do what's fair. There are times when we are faced with a dilemma—want something so much. But, deep down in your stomach, there's a nudge—a 'don't do that' kind of nudge. I must confess, I was unsure…it felt wrong to take the Spirit Jar home. But, on the other hand, I didn't know the history of the artifact or the significance of where it was buried." She shrugged. "Who knew?"

Ray blew out a whoosh of air. "Maybe it's better that we found the Spirit Jar, rather than some unscrupulous treasure seekers, haphazardly digging for items just to sell." He peered over his sunglasses. "I think we all will agree that the sacred place will remain a secret within our family. Storing artifacts in museums preserves some history. But I feel what we are doing, returning the Spirit Jar to its rightful home, is best."

"Absolutely," Laura agreed. She gathered the empty snack bags and stuffed them in her backpack. Observing Annie trotting at Morgan's side, she said, "That salve seems to have worked."

"Yes. It's good medication." Ray said. He rubbed his forehead with the back of his hand. "Guess the best way to do this," he said as he looked up and down the path that hugged the riverbank, "is to walk until we don't see anyone. How does that sound?"

Adjusting her cap, Laura mused silently, "It's going to be hard on those kids if we *do* find someone to claim Annie." Aloud she said, "Sounds like a good idea."

Early fall in the high altitude had introduced chilly days and cold nights. There were only a few people spending the day, fishing along the riverbank. And no one knew anything about a lost dog.

"Guess that's it," Ray said. "And I believe we're getting close to our intended destination." He fingered the trail map from a back pocket.

Laura narrowed her eyes. "Aren't we on the wrong side of the river?"

"You're right," said Ray. He eyed the span of slow-moving water. "Okay, guys, here's a good place to cross." He squatted, picked up a slender stick, and pierced the water. "Only about two feet deep. And," he said as he wagged the stick toward exposed boulders crisscrossing the riverbed, "we could use those as stepping stones to the other side."

In a slightly doubtful tone, Laura said, "I suppose that would work."

Sara took a giant step onto a boulder. Her red rain boots slid on the slippery surface.

"SARA!" shouted Laura as her daughter swayed and bent forward, attempting to keep her balance. Her rigid arms flapped at her sides.

Ray reached out and grabbed her around the waist. "Whoa! I didn't mean for you to be first," he said.

Morgan said, "Hey, Sis, that was entertaining. Whatcha doing for an encore?"

She gave him a withering look and clutched her father's arms. "I don't know, but I'll think of something."

"Up you go, princess," said Ray, lifting Sara onto his shoulders. "Hold tight."

Sara clamped her eyelids and wrapped her arms around his neck. "I'm scared, Daddy," she said.

"Not to worry," said Ray.

Morgan counted aloud. "There's eight of 'em."

"I see," replied Ray. He stood at the edge of the riverbank a moment, before taking the first step.

Morgan said, "Watch this. Here's how it's done." He leaped from rock to rock and sprang to the grassy bank, nailing a perfect landing. Punching the air overhead with his fists, he said, "Piece of cake."

Ray puffed a deep breath. "Here we go," he said, grasping Sara's slippery boots.

When Ray hopped from the last rock to the riverbank, Sara exclaimed, "We made it, Daddy!"

"Piece of cake!" said Ray as he slid Sara from his shoulders.

Not ready to tackle the crossing just yet, Laura sat on a stump. She eyed the flowing water and felt the warmth of Annie's muzzle on her thigh. She chuckled and patted the dog's head. "Are you scared too?"

Morgan, cupped his hands around his mouth and called out, "You can do it, Mom. Just go for it."

Laura stood and squared her shoulders, "Okay girl. Let's do it."

Annie held her head high as she dog-paddled across.

Halfway across, Laura hesitated saying, "Good. Almost there."

Suddenly, her backpack shifted.

Her foot slid sideways on the boulder's slippery surface.

"NOOOO!" she screamed as she toppled into icy water.

"*Mom!*' yelled Morgan.

"OhmiGod! Hang on, honey," Ray yelled. He struggled out of his backpack and parka. And lunged toward the water.

"Mommy," Sara moaned, too frightened to move.

Annie leaped into the water.

Canine instinct urged instant reaction. The dog sank her teeth into something solid, attached to the woman. She pulled toward the man.

Ray grabbed Laura around her torso, and tugged her shivering body onto the riverbank. He quickly removed her water-soaked jacket.

"Morgan, get her boots and socks off," said Ray. *"Hurry!"*

He worked as fast as he could, tugging wet leather footwear and socks off his mother's feet.

"Sara, in my backpack there's a survival blanket, thermal long johns and a Windbreaker. Get them for me," Ray said.

"Here, Dad, take these," said Morgan, handing him the socks that he'd been wearing.

"Good thinking, Son," said Ray. "At least they're dry."

"I…I'm…okay, guys," said Laura through chattering teeth.

"You *will* be as soon as we get you dried out," said Ray.

After changing into the dry clothing, Laura, sat in a patch of sun, clutching the sheer metallic survival blanket around her shoulders.

"The water…" She shivered. "Wasn't deep. I tried to get up. But the stones in the riverbed were slippery. And the current— so strong." Scrubbing her chilled arms she said, "I could have been dragged downriver…"

Giving Annie a tender smile, Laura said, "She saved me."

"She sure did," said Ray. "She's smart, this dog. And mighty brave too."

Morgan sat on a rock near Annie, feeding her pieces of beef

jerky strips. "Here ya go girl. You deserve a reward."

A slight frown clouded Sara's expression as she said, "Mommy? I was thinking that maybe you could put plastic baggies over your socks. You know, cause your boots are wet."

"Great idea, sweetie," said Laura. "They're supposed to be waterproof. But I don't know how waterproof." She paused, looking at her drenched clothing. "I'm sure there's a couple of spare baggies in one of our backpacks."

"How are you doing, honey?" Ray asked. "Feel up to continuing our journey?"

"Yes," Laura said. "Actually, I'm doing great. My hair is almost dry."

"I'm sure glad I had that survival gear along," said Ray.

Laura stood. "So am I," she said.

She gazed up the trail that split a few yards ahead. "Which path do we take?"

Morgan reached into the neck of his sweatshirt and fingered out the string tied to the compass. Studying the instrument lying in his palm, he turned slowly, left then right. "Yup," he said. He pointed toward the split path. "We go left."

Ray smiled at Morgan, pulling the trail map from his back pocket. "Mind if I check?"

"No prob, Dad." He laced his fingers on top of his baseball cap. "Bet you a dollar I'm right."

Ray studied the map.

"You're right-on, my boy," Ray conceded. "About half a mile walk." he tucked the map away and winked at Morgan.

"You owe me a dollar," Morgan called over his shoulder as he jogged up the trail.

Ray turned to Laura and asked, "Sure you're okay, honey?"

Laura gave him a quick hug saying, "I'm okay. *Really.*"

Chapter Twenty-nine

Morgan scrambled up the familiar ridge ahead of the others, climbing onto the crest that overlooked the glade beside the Hawk Valley River where the ancient juniper guarded sacred ground.

Excitement surged through his stomach as he stood a moment, scanning the area below.

He picked his way down the grassy slope. In the shade of the juniper, Morgan slid the backpack straps off his shoulders. Kneeling, he unbuckled the flap and lifted the Spirit Jar from its resting place.

His parents joined him, standing quietly.

Above the timberline, a bald eagle circled a boulder jutting from the mountain's crest. The eagle swept its expansive wings upward and landed, settling its black feathers against its massive body. Soft coos traveled toward the boy kneeling on hallowed ground.

As Morgan held the Spirit Jar in his hands, his emotions split.

"I'm cool with this," he told himself.

Aloud, his throat tight with emotion, he said, "But will I dream of Young Eagle again?"

Annie snuffled the precious object—the Spirit Jar, leaking soft squeaks.

"Hey, girl," said Morgan. "You know, if I hadn't returned, we wouldn't have found you." He massaged her tangled ruff. "So this is *good.*"

Sara ran to his side, clutching a bouquet of leaves tinted gold and bronze.

"We could lay these on the grave," she said. After a moment, she shrugged saying, "They'll probably blow away though."

"That's okay, sweetie," said Laura. "It'll still be a nice gesture."

Morgan's expression turned sober as he walked around the giant juniper and found the place where the Spirit Jar had rested undisturbed for who knows how long.

"Can I have the camp shovel, Dad?"

"Sure. Here you go."

"Can I help," Sara asked.

"In a minute, Sis," Morgan said. He scooped the loose dirt from their previous digging, enlarging the space. Using the side of the shovel, he scraped dirt from the inside wall until he had an almost perfect oval.

"I think you've gone deep enough," said Ray.

Morgan rummaged through his backpack. He pulled out a square piece of wool fabric he'd cut from the corner of the Army blanket he kept rolled inside his sleeping bag. He laid the cloth on the floor of the burial hole.

Sara unzipped her backpack and plucked out the two arrowheads she had wrapped in paper towels. She kissed each one before carefully placing them on the piece of blanket.

Placing the Spirit Jar upon the arrowheads, Morgan murmured, "You're back where you belong."

As he reached for the camp shovel, Morgan's eyes widened.

Across the river, a doe stood statuelike, its round chocolate eyes gazing over the water.

"Is she staring at me?" he wondered silently.

After a moment of sniffing the forest-scented air, her stubby tail quivered, flushing a flock of sparrows from some nearby shrub. The deer lowered her head slowly and sipped from the river.

"Check it out," Morgan whispered.

The animal gracefully lowered her body and stared at the group gathered under the juniper.

Sara cupped her small hands around her mouth and whispered back, "Maybe the deer wants to be included in our ceremony."

Laura did not realize she was holding her breath as she watched the drama across the river. She sucked in air and blew out slowly. Pressing a forefinger against her mouth she said, "Shush, kids, listen." She closed her eyes. "What do you hear?"

"The river?" said Morgan, "that's all I hear."

Sara hugged Annie's neck. "The birds and squirrels aren't talking," she said.

Laura smiled and said, "The forest creatures must be taking a nap!"

Ray chuckled. "Well, guess we better get on with it," he said, nodding toward the doe resting on the riverbank, "before our regal audience leaves."

"Yeah, Morgan," Sara echoed, "before…" Giving her father

a questioning look, she asked, "Daddy, what's 'regal'?"

"It means," Ray said in a quiet voice, "like a princess."

Sara smiled at her father.

"Maybe this princess of the forest wants to witness our little ceremony," Laura said.

"Yeah," said Sara She removed her red rain hat, crushing it against her chest.

Before covering the Spirit Jar, Morgan lifted the backpack and fished the neatly folded apology note from a zippered compartment. Keeping his eyes lowered, he said, "I memorized the note." He hesitated before asking, "Could I just say it to myself?"

"Do what you feel, Son." Ray reached down saying, "Give me your hand." He pulled Morgan to his feet.

"That's perfectly fine," Laura said, circling an arm around Morgan's shoulders, and giving him a quick hug. "We won't peek."

"I know," Morgan sighed. He gave them a weak smile and silently recited the words he had written. He squatted beside the open grave, rolled the paper into a pencil-size cylinder, and tucked it inside the Spirit Jar.

Sara helped her brother scoop dirt over the artifacts. Morgan firmly pressed the mounded soil.

Sara carefully placed her bouquet on the tiny grave.

As Morgan pushed to his feet, a warm breeze brushed his face. The bald eagle rose from the boulder into the pale blue sky, disappearing over the mountain.

Morgan closed his eyes, Young Eagle's bronze face flashed behind his eyelids.

Just then, the doe flicked its ears and plunged into the safety of the thick forest. Squirrels circled tree trunks, scolding in raspy croaks. Blue jays squawked and dove toward the ground, in search of fallen acorns. Sparrows and finches chirped, darting in and out of bushes.

The forest came alive again.

Laura asked in a quite tone, "Morgan, would you like to spend a few moments alone before we start back?"

Morgan shrugged a silent answer. Fumbling with his cap, he said, "This seems so…so final." He stared at the grave, taking his time before he turned and walked away from the sacred ground.

Ray shaded his eyes and looked toward the west, saying, "It'll be dark in a couple of hours. Time to head back."

Sara, tossed a stick. "Look, Annie likes to fetch." She pitched another stick underhanded, and said, "Go get it." The dog retrieved it and laid it at her feet. "See, I taught her."

Morgan reached into a pocket for a piece of jerky. "Here you go, girl."

Leaning against a tree trunk, Morgan clutched his backpack against his chest, fingertips drumming on the canvas fabric. He looked at his dad. "We didn't find anyone who claimed Annie yet," He paused. "And, like you said, we can keep her…Right?"

"Hold on a minute. We better check with Mom about that. If we don't find anyone to claim her, it has to be a family decision."

"Annie would make a great family pet," Laura said. "After what she did this morning? There is no question as to her bravery." She hesitated, casting Morgan and Sara a serious look. "But keep in mind, we could still find someone in camp that lost her." She looked down at the scruffy dog and shook her head. "We'll need to get her to the vet right away. She may need shots."

Sara hiked her shoulders, pressing her hands against her cheeks. "Yikes! Shots!" She grinned and said, "Maybe she'll get a doggie sucker."

Laura chuckled, "Now *that* I've got to see."

Morgan dropped to one knee and hugged Annie around the neck. "I know, we have to try," he said.

Sara laid her cheek on top of the dog's head and tenderly said, "I love you, Annie. I'll keep my fingers crossed."

Laura bit back a smile. Uncertainty clouded her eyes as she coaxed, "Okay, guys, it's time to go."

Annie trotted between Morgan and Sara as they trekked toward the forest trail leading to the campground.

As they entered the shadowy forest, the temperature dipped several degrees.

"Are you kids going to be warm enough?" Laura asked.

A mischievous smile tugged at the corner of Sara's mouth. "I'm almost boiling, Mommy."

"Well, humor me and zip your jacket anyway," said Laura.

"I'm fine," Morgan quietly replied. He stopped and looked over his shoulder in the direction of the river. "Guess this is good bye," he whispered.

"I'll remember Young Eagle—my dream brother—forever," Morgan told himself. "The stuff he told me about his tribe. The exciting adventures. And my vision quest to seek my guardian animal spirit." Morgan smiled to himself, thinking, *"And I am Standing Bear."*

After a minute, he turned and marched up the trail. Annie, not wanting to be left behind, followed on his heels.

Suddenly, Laura's intuition clicked in. "Morgan's dreams with Young Eagle have truly ended. The Spirit Jar is connected to Morgan and the Native American boy, in some mysterious way," she thought. "And what about Annie? Will we find her family and have to leave her behind too?" Sorrow leaked into her thoughts. She drew a deep breath and turned toward Ray.

Seeing her sad expression, Ray said, "Don't worry, Morgan's okay. He just needs a few minutes alone."

"I know," she replied softly.

"Let's hit the trail," Ray said. "We can't let him get too far ahead."

Hearing Annie's bark reverberating through the forest, Laura said, "Good to hear that sound. Morgan must be close."

"There he is," said Sara. She swooped off her red rain hat and waved it over her head. "He's up there, standing on a rock by that big tree."

Squinting into the shadowy forest, Ray said, "I see him."

಄ಃ಄   ಄ಃ಄   ಄ಃ಄

Dusk had claimed the forest by the time they reached the outskirts of the campground.

Morgan clicked on a flashlight and led the way. Over his shoulder, he called, "I see the path to our campsite ahead." Reassuring his parents, as well as himself, he added, "Told you guys not to worry."

"*Duh,*" said Sara as she rolled her eyes and skipped ahead, Annie on her heels. "Guess you think you're a genius."

"Now, now, princess," Ray said. "Your brother is good at reading the compass. We gotta give him that much credit."

"Well done, Morgan," Laura said, casting him a bright smile.

"Thanks, Mom."

Laura struck a match and lit the lantern wick. "Sara help me get supper together. And please wash your hands first. I'm going to change into some other clothes."

"Okay, Mommy."

Shrugging off his backpack straps, Ray gave Morgan a confiding wink and said, "I wasn't worried a bit."

Morgan delivered a broad grin. "Thanks, Dad." He crouched beside the fire pit and scooped up fistfuls of twigs. Popping noises sounded as he slowly emptied his cargo over crumpled newspaper.

Hunching over Morgan's shoulder, Sara said, "Got enough twigs?"

"Jeez, Sara. You don't need to holler," said Morgan. He massaged his ear. "You scared me. Go away. I can handle this."

"Sorreee," she said, and flounced off toward the washbasin. In a singsong tone, she added, "Excuse *me*."

"Dad, should I put a log on," Morgan asked, sweeping a hand over the fire pit, "before you light this?"

Ray dried his hands and joined him. "Looks good. You can put a couple of the smaller logs on after it gets going." He crouched by the stacked rocks bordering the fire pit, scratched a wooden kitchen match against the inner ring, and held the flame to a corner of the crumpled paper.

They watched as yellow flames slowly spread and licked the dry kindling.

As he pushed to his feet, Ray said, "How about we wait till morning to continue the search for Annie's family?"

A boisterous, unanimous yes resounded from the youngsters. They shared a broad smile and the same thought: *"We get to keep her a few more hours."*

Laura and Ray, also shared a thought: *"Are we prolonging heartbreak? Is Annie just a visitor—for one night?"*

Annie's future with the Shephard family teetered on fate.

Chapter Thirty

Hot beef stew scented the evening air as Laura set a cast-iron pot on the picnic table.

"Sara, please fill this with water," Laura said, handing her a chipped white enamelware pitcher that had belonged to her grandmother.

Laura spooned helpings into unmatched "garage sale" bowls. "Okay, guys, it's dinner."

"Mmm, smells good," Ray said, tearing open a crusty sour-dough roll.

Water sloshed over the top of the pitcher as Sara plunked it on the table. "Oops! Sorreee." She dabbed at driblets of water with a paper napkin. "Mommy, I'm not too hungry." Her nose crinkled as she said, "Just a smidge, please."

"Yeah, right," Morgan snickered. "Bet you'll be ready to eat when the bag of marshmallows comes out."

Laura laughed. "You mean you're not having seconds of this lovely Dinty Moore stew," she said, peering into the cooking pot and arching an eyebrow, "that I slaved over, getting the temperature just right?" Eyes glistening in amusement, she scooped a dab of the thick, gravy-soaked meat and vegetables into a bowl.

Casting her brother a smug expression, Sara said, "Thanks, Mommy."

"You're welcome. Now, let's eat."

"This stuff *is* tasty," Ray said. He winked at Laura. "I'm enjoying it."

Buttering a roll, Laura replied, "Camping menus beg for stew or chili."

Ray chuckled. "Always a good choice."

Turning toward Morgan, Laura asked, "Say, how do you feel about today? I mean about burying the Spirit Jar?"

"I've been thinking...if we hadn't come back to return the Spirit Jar, we wouldn't have found Annie." A smile curved his mouth. "So I'm okay with what we did."

Sara looked over her shoulder at Annie, lying near the table. "We had fun today, huh, girl?" Sara's expression sobered. "And you saved Mommy."

"She sure did," said Ray.

"I am such a klutz," said Laura, shaking her head. "The water wasn't deep, but sure was cold."

"Good thing Dad carries emergency stuff," said Morgan.

The lantern flame grew momentarily, encouraging shadows to waltz around the table. The evening campfire crackled, spreading the turpentine aroma of burning pitch through the chill night air.

Laura glanced around the table and smiled. "Isn't this cozy?"

Ray steepled his fingers under his chin. His dark eyes mirrored the lantern's flame.

"You know, today will be one of my favorite memories. Sara

surrendering the arrowheads and Morgan placing the Spirit Jar into the earth made my heart sing."

He shook his head slowly. "Now that image is a…a real treasure."

Joy fluttered through the space below her heart as Laura listened to her husband's revelation. In a tone barely above a whisper, she said, "You are so right, my love." She reached over and patted his shoulder. "It *was* a perfect day."

Morgan's gaze settled on the diminishing flames in the fire pit. "If I never dream of Young Eagle again," he said as he slid the journal toward himself, "I'll write about him in here." His expression turned wistful. "Adventures with my dream brother," he added silently.

Ray and Laura shared a smile.

Annie chased a plate of stew under the table. She planted a front paw in the middle to anchor it and licked until the paper turned limp.

Sara clamped her hands over her mouth, stifling a string of giggles, as she bent down to watch.

"What's so funny?" Morgan asked. He leaned down toward the seat and lifted the table covering.

"Hey, girl," said Morgan. "Good to the last…

"There's something…"

Morgan grabbed a flashlight from the table and switched it on.

Squinting at the ground near his foot, he sucked a breath.

His pulse quickened.

"*You guys won't believe this!*" he cried, his expression was full of surprise. "Seriously, *this is so weird!*"

"Believe what?" Ray asked, setting his coffee mug down.

"Mom! Dad! Look under the table by my foot," said

Morgan.

Laura quickly shifted her feet, propping them on the picnic bench.

"*OhmiGod!*" she cried. "*Is it moving?*"

"Trust me, Mom," Morgan laughed. "Nothing's alive."

Issuing a throaty chuckle, Ray quirked an eyebrow toward Morgan and said, "Better not be."

Sara scrambled off her seat for a better view.

"Don't touch 'em, Sara," Morgan warned. He grabbed a roll of paper towels and tore off a sheet. He reached down and carefully laid the objects on the towel. An elated expression claimed his eyes as he produced two flint arrowheads, in perfect condition.

"Oh my!" Laura said. "Where did *they* come from?" She touched one with a forefinger. "Maybe someone lost them."

Ray peered at the arrowheads resting in Morgan's hands. "I don't know what to think. I'm astonished."

"I know why they're here," Sara said, shrugging a shoulder. "It's a reward—because we put the Spirit Jar back." She flipped a stray curl behind an ear. "And the other arrowheads too."

Laura looked at Sara. "You think?"

Massaging an earlobe, Ray said, "Strange. But she could be right."

Morgan brushed specks of dirt from the arrowheads. Slowly shaking his head, he said, "This is so totally awesome."

"So, can we keep these ones?" Sara asked.

"Yes," Laura said. She winked at Ray. "I believe it's okay for us to take them home."

"ALL RIGHT!" Morgan shouted.

Alarmed by the boy's sudden outcry, Annie bristled and backed away from the table, squeaking softly.

"Oh, Morgan," Sara said. "You scared her." She bent over and softly patted her hands together murmuring, "It's okay, girl."

"Sorry, Annie. I just got excited," said Morgan.

୯୬୭ ୯୬୭ ୯୬୭

After dinner, the family gathered around the fire pit and toasted marshmallows.

Morgan stared into the flames, listening to his parents speculate about the mysterious appearance of the two arrowheads. He had his own theory—that his dream brother had performed a magical act and left them as a gift.

"After all," he mused silently, they were near *my* foot just waiting for me to notice."

୯୬୭ ୯୬୭ ୯୬୭

Late night mist hovered over the forest floor. A three-quarter moon rose, illuminating the surrounding pines to a spooky, pearl gray sheen. Logs burned to skeletal charcoal and split with a snap, sinking into hot coals. Conversation dwindled, yawning spread from one to another, and eyelids began to droop.

"I don't know about you guys, but I'm ready to call it a day," Ray said.

"It's time," Laura agreed.

Annie rose and followed Sara. "Don't worry, girl. We'll find a place for you to sleep. Mommy, Annie's afraid." She stroked the dog's head. "Maybe she knows she's just visiting us. But *really* wants to come to *our* house to live."

"We'll see what happens tomorrow, princess," said Ray.

"Okay," Sara sighed. "Could I make a bed for her?"

From inside the van, Laura answered, "Sure, sweetie. Give me a minute." Crawling toward the back of the car, she found a tattered afghan. "Here you go." As an afterthought she added, "Have Morgan spread a few pine needles before you lay it down. She'll sleep warm as toast."

"Thanks, Mommy," said Sara. Hugging the blanket to her chest, she asked, "Daddy, where's a good place for Annie's bed?"

"Next to the tent would be a good spot."

After a pad was prepared for orphaned Annie, Sara crawled to the middle of the makeshift bed. She sat cross-legged, urging in a soft tone, "Come, girl." she gently patted the afghan. "See how nice it is?"

The dog took a tentative step onto the blanket. After a few curious sniffs, she collapsed, ejecting a soft woof. She lowered her muzzle onto her crossed front paws, her gold-flecked eyes blinking in the darkness.

Morgan sucked a quick breath and turned away. Pure love for this dog threatened to burst from his chest.

Straightening a corner of the blanket, Sara said, "She likes her bed."

Laura's eyes clouded. "Don't forget," she cautioned, "first thing tomorrow morning we have to check around the camp for her family."

A resigned, "We know," issued from the youngsters.

Ray yawned and stretched. "Annie seems content to sleep outside," he said.

Tossing Sara a towel, Laura said, "Let's get to the restroom." She nodded to Ray, "There are towels and soap on your sleeping bags." In a firm tone, she added, "Morgan, don't forget to brush your teeth."

"No problem, Mom." Swinging a plastic bag overhead, he called out, "Got everything right here."

Ray retrieved two towels and draped one around his neck. He tossed the other to Morgan. "You go ahead. I'll wash up when you get back."

"Okay," answered Morgan. He bounced the beam of his flashlight off tree trunks as he wandered toward the restroom building.

A scuffling noise near the path brought him to an abrupt stop.

Goose bumps prickled the back of his neck.

"What's that?" he muttered.

Morgan jerked a beam of light toward the sound.

A raccoon poked its head around a trash can. Dark eyes blinked in the bright light. Like a giant slug, it lumbered through dry leaves and into the forest.

"Ha!" cried Morgan. "Just a raccoon."

He entered the dimly lit restroom. Peering into a mirror coated with dust, he held the flashlight below his chin. Pulling a long face, he frowned. His reflection transformed into a monster's mask as he sucked in his lips. After practicing another odd expression, he lay the flashlight on the grimy sink.

"I wasn't that scared outside," Morgan told himself. Aloud, he said, "Yeah, right! You were for a second."

Later, sprawled on his sleeping bag, Morgan closed his eyes. In a husky voice, he said, "Thanks, Dad, for bringing me here." He clutched the Army blanket to his chest, fingering the missing corner. The square he had cut out to lay beneath the Spirit Jar. Sighing, he rolled onto his side.

"You're welcome, Son," said Ray. He smiled into the darkness. "Glad Mom and I could help you out. See you in the morning."

"Night, Dad."

Morgan closed his eyes, visualizing the two arrowheads he had found under the picnic table, tucked in his backpack.

"They *are* magical," Morgan thought as sleep engulfed him, and a dream rolled into his unconscious mind.

Chapter Thirty-one

*F*alling *at a terrifying speed, Morgan's stomach lurched.*

"No, no! Pleeeease no," Morgan moaned as he gulped for air. Gusts buffeted his face and pitched him upside down.

His panic vanished in a dream-moment when his guardian animal spirit, the huge grizzly bear materialized. Shaggy brown paws gently enfolded him and calmed his lurching heart.

Morgan was safe.

And then, as the wind shriveled, the animal disappeared.

"Thank you, guardian animal spirit," Morgan shouted in a dream voice.

He pressed his arms against his sides and lifted his chin. His eyes widened as a bald eagle appeared. Its dark brown wings spread wide. The huge bird glided high above him.

Tears stained Morgan's eyes as he struggled to keep the eagle in sight.

Fear, like a jagged piece of glass, pierced his chest when the bird suddenly swooped downward and gripped his deerskin shirt with its talons. Its clawed beak parted, exposing a yellow snakelike tongue.

Shivering, Morgan tightened his eyelids, attempting to erase the nightmare image.

But the massive bird hauled its human cargo, skimming tree tops, until it landed with a gentle thud in a meadow. It released Morgan and hopped onto a large boulder.

Telepathic messages from the eagle, seeped into Morgan's sleeping mind.

"Open your eyes, Standing Bear," the bird seemed to say. "Do not be afraid."

Morgan peered at the feathered creature and knew it was his dream brother, Young Eagle.

"It is time, Standing Bear," said Young Eagle." I have something to tell you.

"Upon my death, long, long ago, the Spirit Jar was prepared to hold my cremation ashes. When it was unearthed and taken from sacred ground, my spirit wandered in restless confusion, searching.

"Then a miracle occurred. Our souls connected in your dreams. And now, my spirit is at rest again. Returned to sacred ground."

Air stirred as the eagle slowly flapped its massive wings and lifted heavily from the boulder.

As the dream vision evaporated, Morgan heard the voice of his dream brother: "You are brave, Standing Bear. Our time together has ended. But remember the legend of my grandfather, Chief White Feather."

Morgan lay motionlessly, in the pre-dawn, recalling the details of his dream.

"Did I get it?" he said quietly. "Could it be true—the chief's grandson?! Mr. Harold did say there were three survivors—Chief White Feather, his son, and grandson."

Deep in his gut, Morgan knew. He knew without a doubt that, Young Eagle was the surviving grandson.

"This is so totally awesome," he said through clenched teeth.

Shivering, he burrowed into his sleeping bag. "Should I tell Mom and Dad?" he wondered silently. "No. Not yet. Maybe later."

Morgan's throat tightened at the thought of Young Eagle vanishing from his dreams.

"I will miss you," he whispered.

He slithered further into his sleeping bag. "But," Morgan thought, "I have the magical arrowheads and the bow and arrow set to remember you. And I'll write about these trips in my journal—everything. Can't wait till I get home and tell the guys about this. They'll never believe it. They definitely won't believe that I have a picture of Young Eagle—proof that he *was* real!"

❧   ❧   ❧

Sunlight piercing the windshield and sporadic thumps on the roof of the van woke Laura. "What is that noise?" she wondered. She flipped onto her back. Through slit eyelids she saw two squirrels scamper across the windshield. She chuckled. "You little scamps startled me."

Feathery, gray tails floated above their rounded backs as they scurried from sight.

"I'm definitely wide awake now," she murmured.

Laura slid the side door open slowly, tugged on her slippers, and stepped into crisp morning air.

"Good morning, love," Ray said, handing her a mug of steaming coffee. "Sara still asleep?"

"I think so," said Laura. She sipped the hot brew and held the mug between her chilled hands. A smile of approval crinkled her eyes. "You make good camp coffee, my dear." She huddled into her down-filled jacket and moved close to the fire. "How about Morgan, still asleep?"

Ray chuckled. "Conked out. I think he was super tired after all the mental anguish he suffered...and the traumatic lake incident." He picked up a piece of kindling and poked at the red coals. "Last time I looked, he was a lump in the middle of his sleeping bag. The kid finally relaxed."

Laura slipped an arm around Ray's waist and leaned into him. He smelled like wood smoke and fresh mountain air. She nodded toward the edge of the tent, where Annie lay dozing in the morning sun.

"Do you think we'll find her owners?" she asked.

Ray sighed and lowered his head. "I don't know. Sure going to be hard on this family if we do."

"I know," she murmured.

A few minutes later, Annie whined a greeting when Morgan crawled out of the tent. Through a yawn he asked, "Hey, girl, you doing okay?" He leaned over and said, "You know what? I hope we can take you home with us."

After breakfast the family walked through the campground, asking everyone if they lost a dog. With each negative response, Morgan gave Sara a broad smile.

Laura said, "Let's visit the store and say good-bye to Mr. Harold. If there's anyone around the store, maybe you kids could ask if they know her?"

Morgan answered in a hesitant tone, "Guess so."

Folding her arms behind her back, Sara crossed her fingers. "I hope we don't find *anyone* who knows her," she said.

❧   ❧   ❧

Mr. Harold's craggy face beamed as Ray and Laura entered the store.

"Howdy, folks. Didn't expect you back so soon. What can I do ya for?"

"It's good to see you, Mr. Harold," Ray responded, removing his sunglasses. He pinched the bridge of his nose. "Our plans were changed a bit."

A smile pulled at her mouth as Laura shook Mr. Harold's gnarled hand. She would rather not have to ask, but knew she must. "We were wondering…have you heard of any lost dogs lately?"

Mr. Harold raked his swollen, arthritic fingers through his wavy gray hair and answered in his slow drawl, "Well, can't say as I have." His permanently creased brow furrowed more deeply. "Why'd you ask—you folks lose a pet?"

"No, not us. But we have a beauty outside," Ray responded. "Came across her while we were hiking. We brought her back to camp, thought we could find her family."

"She was somewhat dehydrated and hungry," said Laura. Slowly shaking her head she added, "Poor thing, lying there near the hiking path—as if she had just given up." She smiled thinking, "Or waiting for us to rescue her?"

"Sorry, Missus," said Mr. Harold. "Can't recall anyone asking after a lost animal."

Out of the corner of her eye, Laura saw Sara's face plastered against the front window. "As much as we would like to keep her," Laura said, "we better ask one more place."

"Huh? Where else?" Ray asked.

"The lake. You know, where we had our picnic and you guys swam," said Laura.

Ray narrowed his eyes, removed his red baseball cap and massaged his neck. "Yeah, you're right." He glanced at the window. Sara's face had disappeared.

As Mr. Harold ambled toward the door, he remarked, "Sorry I couldn't be more help to you folks." The cowbell clanged as he opened the door. "You say she's outside?"

Morgan and Sara sat huddled on the log bench. Annie lay at their feet. "Any news about a lost dog?" Morgan asked, his tone bordered with hope.

"Not a word, Son," Ray said with a wink. "Can't say I'm disappointed."

"We're going to inquire one more place," Laura said, sitting next to Morgan. "Remember the lake where we had the picnic?" She circled an arm around his shoulders. "If no one… well, then I'll feel we have done everything we can. Okay?"

Morgan mumbled, "Yeah, guess we have to look everywhere." His narrow shoulders sagged in a deep sigh. "This stinks," he told himself.

Sara knelt beside the dog she now loved. "Oh, Annie," she said.

Ray leaned over Sara, his hands braced on his thighs. "Best we be on our way, princess," he said.

"Mr. Harold, so good to see you again," Laura said.

"We'll be back, sir," Ray said, reaching out to shake hands. "You can count on it." He grasped Sara's outstretched hands and swung her from the porch.

"Whee! Do that again, Daddy," Sara said as she clambered up onto the porch.

"One more time, and then we have to get going," said Ray.

Mr. Harold chuckled. "Well now, you folks have a safe trip home."

"Oh," Laura said as she stood a moment at the edge of the porch, "before I forget, Mr. Harold, do you recall the names of Chief White Feather's son and grandson?"

Mr. Harold tugged an earlobe. "Recollect I do, Missus. Let's see...get 'em in the right order." He paused a long while. "His son, I believe, was called Black Horse and his grandson...oh yes, Young Eagle."

Startled to hear the name spoken by someone else, Laura sucked a quick breath. She closed her eyes, too shaken to speak.

Morgan ducked his head.

His heart lurched.

"Gotta tell them now, about the picture," he thought. "Just hope they don't freak out."

"What?" Ray asked incredulously. His eyes narrowed. "Are you sure about those names, sir?"

"Yes sirree. No doubt about it," said Mr. Harold. Before entering his store he turned and said, "Hope to see you folks next year."

"Let's sit," Ray said to Morgan. "How about it? Got something on your mind?"

"Yeah, been meaning to tell you," Morgan said. He dropped to the porch, clamping his arms around his folded legs and resting his chin on his knees.

Laura sank to the log bench. Thoughts weaved through her mind: "Spirit Jar connected...Morgan's dreams about the

Native American boy, Young Eagle, the surviving grandson...
spirit crashed into his unconscious...unearthed pottery jar."

She leaned forward, sandwiching her hands between her
quaking knees, and asked, "Did you have another dream,
Morgan?"

He nodded, whispering, "Yes."

He described his final Young Eagle dream—every detail.

"The dream was scary at first," said Morgan.

"A huge eagle grabbed my deerskin shirt, with its talons,
that's what I was wearing, and carried me to a meadow. The
bird spoke, not aloud words, but words inside my dreaming
mind," Morgan said. Pausing a moment he continued. "I...I
knew for sure the bird was really, Young Eagle. The eagle told
me not to be afraid. It called me by my Native American name,
Standing Bear."

Ray frowned, "I'm lost here," he said.

"Standing Bear?" Laura said.

"I better fill you in on how I got that name," Morgan said.

His parents answered together, "Please do."

"Well, in one of my dreams, Young Eagle guided me into
a vision quest. And a gigantic grizzly bear appeared. I knew
right away he was my guardian animal spirit. And the name
Standing Bear entered the picture." Morgan smiled, "I feel
good about that.

"Young Eagle explained that a long time ago the Spirit Jar
was prepared for his cremation ashes. And that when I dug
it up, his spirit wandered in restless confusion. But he said a
miracle happened—our souls connected. And now his spirit is
at rest. He told me I was brave and to remember the legend of

his grandfather, Chief White Feather.

"Mom, Dad, there's something else," said Morgan. Clearing his throat, he began, "Now this will sound like I'm hallucinating. But trust me, I'm not. *Really.*"

Sara jiggled Laura's forearm. "What's ha-lu—" she frowned unable to finish pronouncing the word.

"Kind of like imaginary, sweetie," said Laura. She searched for a better way to explain. "You know, something that is invisible, but you were positive you saw or heard it—like a real person or real object or a real sound."

"Oh," Sara answered, still looking confused.

"Sorry for the interruption, Morgan," said Laura.

"Go on, Son," said Ray.

Morgan's expression turned solemn as he spoke to his parents. "When I tell you this…well, you're just going to have to see it to believe it. Promise to keep an open mind?"

"You have our word," said Ray.

Morgan pushed to his feet, unable to sit still.

Sara gave him a wary look, snuggling Annie for comfort.

"Okay," Morgan began, "remember the copy of the photograph of the Native Americans I got from the library book? You know, the one of the boy and older guy?"

"Yes, of course," said Laura.

"Tacked to your bedroom door, isn't it?" Ray asked.

"Yeah, that one," said Morgan. "The boy's face seemed familiar. So the other day I checked him out with my magnifying glass." He drew a deep breath, releasing it through puffed lips. "And, this is hard to believe, but, he is Young Eagle."

Laura blinked, "*What?!* she cried.

"Are you sure about that?" said Ray.

"Yes, Dad, I'm positive. Even though there's no information anywhere on the picture, when or where it was taken, I'm sure it's Young Eagle and his grandfather, Chief White Feather. Lots of photographs of different Native American tribes were in that book."

Morgan watched his parents exchange uneasy glances.

"Since you put it that way," said Laura, after some thought, "sure. That's possible. According to the legend, they did exist." She shook her head slowly. "It's all so like," she said, smiling and raising her eyebrows, "synchronicity."

Frustrated at another long word, Sara whined, "Mommy, what does *that* mean?"

"Oh, okay, sweetie," said Laura. She bit the corner of her bottom lip, thinking of a simple explanation. "Ah! Well from the day you and Morgan uncovered the arrowheads and the Spirit Jar, many strange and unusual things have happened—your brother's dreams with Young Eagle and what he learned from him, our returning those artifacts to sacred ground, and the distinct possibility that our trip to the library somehow led Morgan to a photograph of Young Eagle and Chief White Feather." She drew a deep breath, releasing it slowly. "All those events are connected somehow."

"Thanks," Sara responded, her expression puzzled. "I guess I sort of understand."

Ray chuckled, turning to Morgan. "Sounds like you have thought a lot about this."

"It all fits, Dad. Think about it," Morgan said. Frowning he added. "But I'll miss Young Eagle in my dreams, you know?" He smiled to himself, musing silently, "My dream brother."

"Yes, I'm sure you will," said Ray. He reached down to help Laura to her feet. "But who knows? Maybe someday you will meet another Young Eagle." He gave his son a warm smile and said, "Maybe an earthly one?"

"That could happen," Laura agreed. "the unusual events of the past weeks remind us that not everything needs to have a tidy explanation." She paused. "But I do believe you were destined to do exactly what you did—unearth the Spirit Jar."

Slipping into his backpack straps, Ray grinned. "You sure will have a great story to tell your children."

Morgan flushed pink. "Sure, Dad."

Chapter Thirty-two

A few minutes past noon, the Shephard family arrived at Crystal Lake. The sun, glancing off the glossy deep, blue surface teared the eyes. A few people were fishing from the bank. Some perched on canvas stools, humped over bamboo poles, staring hopefully at red and white plastic bobbins attached to filament fishing line. Others lounged in folding aluminum lawn chairs, fishing poles propped on a nearby rock or log.

Morgan stood at the water's edge a moment, silently thanking Young Eagle for rescuing him that day. There was no monster-creature submerged below the surface. He was certain his dream brother had pulled him to safety.

"Let's get this over with," Ray said, his voice tight with emotion.

"Yeah," Morgan groaned. "C' mon, Annie, let's go for a walk." Hearing the word "walk" sparked her canine instinct. Tail wagging and whimpering, she begged to get started.

"Sara and I will stay here," said Laura, glancing away from the lake. She locked her arms over her stomach and nodded toward a stand of pines. "Up there."

Sara breathed, "I love you" into Annie's twitching ear. Crossing her fingers, she turned and reluctantly followed her mother.

Each negative response to Ray's query triggered a yip of joy through Laura. At the end of the lakeside trail, Morgan raised his fists overhead and punched the air.

Ray cupped his hands around his mouth and shouted, "SHE'S OURS!"

"Oh, Mommy, I was holding my breath," said Sara. "So *now* can we take Annie home?"

"It appears so, sweetie," said Laura. She gently pulled Sara against her thigh. "Guess whomever she belonged to has left the area. Probably thought they would never find her in these woods."

Sara wiggled from her mother's hand and tipped her head toward the sky. She closed her eyes and whispered, "Thank you."

A broad smile split Morgan's face as he ran toward his mother and Sara. Breathless, he said, "Guess what! No one knows who Annie's family is. Not one of those guys ever saw her before." Bracing his hands on his knees and gasping for air, he added, "Said they would have remembered *her*."

Ray eased onto a boulder and swiped a sleeved arm across his forehead. "We have a dog in the family."

Sara knelt beside Annie and said, "You'll like our house, girl." She looked at Laura. "Mommy, could we get one of those doggie beds?"

"We have to buy Annie a dish," said Morgan. A slight frown rippled across his brow. "She'll need two dishes. One for water and one for food."

Ray massaged Annie's ears. "We'll get her outfitted when we get home. Don't worry."

Morgan tossed a stick, "Go get it, girl."

Grabbing another stick, Sara protested, "Let me. I taught her to fetch."

"Work it out, guys," Ray said.

"Okay, okay," said Morgan. "But she doesn't need to be so possessive. Annie belongs to all of us. Besides, when we get home I'll teach her all kinds of tricks and stuff."

Digging into her backpack for grahams and dried fruit, Laura said, "Let's have a snack before hiking back to the campsite." She glanced toward Annie and added. "A celebration in honor of the newest family member."

Ray pulled water bottles from his backpack. "Got any of that beef jerky left?" he asked Morgan.

"Two strips. Right here in my jacket pocket."

As they snacked, Ray suggested they hike an alternate trail to the campground. Studying the map, he assured them, "Not much out of our way. You all up for it?"

"Can I see the map, Dad?" asked Morgan.

"Sure," said Ray. "In fact why don't you chart our course?"

"Great. No problem."

"Do you think we have enough time before it gets dark?" Laura asked, peering at her wristwatch.

"Yeah, we can make it," said Ray.

A short bark from Annie settled it.

"Good girl," Morgan said. "We're ready. C' mon, Sara."

Ray nodded toward Morgan and said, "Lead the way, my man."

❧   ❧   ❧

Dusk saturated the forest as the hikers trudged up the last incline leading into the campsite.

"You did good, Son," said Ray, "kept us on a true course back to camp."

Morgan removed his baseball cap. Sweeping an exaggerated bow he said, "Thank you, thank you—no applause please!"

Laura chuckled at the gesture. "I have to agree," she said. "Now how about some dinner?"

"I'm starved," said Sara.

Ray reached over and massaged Laura's shoulder. "I'll get a fire going," he said.

❧   ❧   ❧

Around the campfire after dinner, they all agreed that Annie was an unexpected gift—a treasure. And that she was lying in their path, waiting to be rescued—the final bit of synchronicity in the chain of mysterious events surrounding the Spirit Jar.

Serendipity at work?

Maybe.

Annie, her back to the fire pit, sat on her haunches, staring into the dark.

Her floppy ears twitched at sounds only she could hear.

Early the next morning, the Shephard family broke camp and left for home.

The End

Epilogue

As Morgan suspected, he never dreamt of Young Eagle again. But he wrote in his journal often, referring to himself as Standing Bear. He needed to record every detail of the odyssey—the adventure that he believed changed his destiny. There was no logical explanation to the mysterious events that took place during the two camping trips.

Did Morgan meet an "earthly" friend resembling Young Eagle?

He did.

Well, not exactly.

His roommate in college, a Native American, became his close friend and confidant. Over the years, Morgan shared the Spirit Jar episode and Young Eagle dreams with his friend.

Annie blended into their lives, remaining happy and healthy for many years.

The two "magical arrowheads" found a place of honor on the fireplace mantle, as well as the miniature bow and arrow set.

Influenced by his vivid dreams of that late summer, when he was twelve, Morgan read numerous books on the subject of Native American history. In college he majored in sciences that guided him into a career he loved. As an anthropologist, he was often called on for his expertise in the search for the origins, customs, and cultural development of humankind.

ISBN 142512115-2

9 781425 121150